MAUD'S HOUSE
by
William Gough

144 PAGES

Maud's House, was first published by Breakwater Books in
1984.
© William Gough 1984
The next edition was published by
Hounslow Press in 1987
© William Gough 1987

ISBN: 978-1-4357-4533-9
William Gough ©2008-07-17
http://williamgough.icopyright.com

MAUD'S HOUSE

by

William Gough

"To my father – Doctor Jim"

Prologue

Maud was sleeping.

She, a little girl, felt the warmth of the feathers in the bed and she dreamed she was floating in a river.

From somewhere she heard a song – "In the Sweet By and By."

She followed the music in her sleep and the moon rose over the river for her.

The moonbeams dusted over a little man.

He was short and fat and naked and he played the saw.

He smiled at Maud and pointed. When she looked to see what he was pointing at, the river took her and spilled her towards the shore.

She climbed from the wave and snow drifted with sand.

Behind the snow she could see a light.

The light shone from a small white house.

Chapter One

The first time Maud saw the house was in winter. The sleigh had just dropped her off at the gate and with a creaking of wood on snow it slid away. Maud's nostrils widened as cold fresh air moved in, replacing the warm smell of leather and harness.

The clop of the horse's hooves was dampened by snow and by distance. All the ride she had snuggled into her wrapping of grey blankets and let the flannel rub along her cheek. It seemed like she'd walked out of home years ago instead of just a morning earlier.

Now, as she looked at the house atop an icy hill, she began to have doubts which lasted until she forced herself into action.

"If you goes," said her father, "never set back home again." Then he softened. "It's still not too late to change your mind. What about if Mother gets sick, or one of the young ones?"

Now she hesitated in front of the new door. At home she'd have just walked right into any house. No need t'knock when she knew everyone. But here she stood in front of the kitchen door and wondered what to do. Perhaps they uses the front door here. I needs to go around.

From the hen house she could hear clucking and then an abrupt squawking which died down. Rat, thought Maud. The house had a little bit of paint peeling near the door. Poor job of painting - a lazy man's strokes. She reached up and knocked. Although it was only twilight and no real need t'burn kerosene, someone inside the house was carrying a lamp through the kitchen and, as the door opened, the soft yellow folded over grey. Maud looked up and saw the most beautiful woman she had ever seen. It was like lookin' at a delicate tea cup she'd seen in the merchant's house once. Fragile and gentle. Light would shine through and you were scared to touch. The woman at the door was like that teacup and it seemed, if she walked in front of the sun, the light would shine right through her. Her bones'd glow hollow as a sparrow's. She was tall and had a neck as white and soft as feathers. Her hair was faded gold, of a pastel that Maud had never seen before.

"I'm here about the job, ma'am."

"My name is Mrs. Sheppard. Come in and warm from the cold."

"Is there still a job?"

"You haven't run away from home?"

They paused just before going into the parlour. Maud noticed that Mrs. Sheppard had to keep ducking so that she wouldn't hit her head on the ceiling. No wonder she stuck her neck up high when she got a chance to look outside.

"No ma'am. I left home. I walked out of somewhere I didn't want to be, and that's a far different thing than runnin' away from home. I told them I was leavin."

Bessie Sheppard paused and sized her up. "Come on in and meet the Skipper. He's the one who decides if you'll get the job."

In the parlour their lamp spread a circle of light over a small varnished table where a lace swan was swimming. Starched with sugar, its webbed doily feet dyed with food colouring, it looked like a candy rich enough to hurt your teeth at the first bite.

The travelling circle warms a black and scarred pedal-driven organ. In the corner near the window yellow light is mixed with grey on an old man. His face looks to be two colours until the lamplight is full and Mrs. Sheppard pulls the curtains.

Maud looks at the hands holding an ebony cane. The hands are thick and full of blue snakes that crawl under his skin. He grips the cane and rocks it back and forth. The trousers are black and the crotch is held by half-closed buttons. His jacket is old and once was grey but round his neck the shirt is buttoned perfectly. There's no collar and his neck scrawns out, hung down with folds of loose skin. Grey stubble covers his face. His mouth is strong and carved in at the corners where small brown stains have leaked tobacco juice. His eyes are dead and grey blue, misted in by cataracts, and float around in tiny circles. They bob and pitch like a buoy on a windy day.

"She got heavy steps, be she a large girl?"

"No, Skipper, she just looks strong and able for the tasks."

"Her name is...?"

"Maud, an' pleased to meet you, Sir..."

"Your handshake is certain. Would it embarrass you to look after an old man like me? Bessie here is family and she shouldn't. Family by marriage. We'll give you room and board found and ten dollars a month."

"When can I start?"

"Why d'ye want the job?"

"I needs the money t'live."

"You could have stayed at home."

"I wants me own life."

Bessie looks towards the Skipper. "She wants something that I can understand. I went in service..."

"Different. You went to Boston and in service with a teacher. That's an education...that's not work."

Maud dares to ask Bessie a question. "You been to Boston? To the States?"

"Yes," and Bessie smiles into the lamplight. "An' there I learned..."

The Skipper interrupts. "Maud your name is? Maud, do y'know how to cook? I haven't seen a thing these last years. Not even the hand before me face. It all looks milk. Like streamers o' clouds up in the sky. Now 'tis all gone grey an' I don't need people who nod. I needs t'hear the words and I needs t'hear the voice."

"Yes."

"Then go to the kitchen an' get some supper. 'Tis tea time an' I'm hungry."

Maud goes out to the kitchen where it's almost dark. The only light comes in thin squares from cracks in the stove. She finds a kerosene lamp, looks at the chimney and, picking up a cloth, runs it through until the glass is shiny. The wick is blunted, black and ragged so she trims it and then, reaching on top of the warmer, finds large heavy wood kitchen matches and strikes one on the sole of her boot. The lamp lights up a green kitchen and shows a brand new bamboo framed "Bless This House." The letters are huge and all a-glitter and Maud pauses to admire it. In the pantry it's cold and Maud finds some bologna, a few potatoes, some beet. At least someone thinks ahead around here. They brought in a bit from the root cellar.

Soon the smell of bologna burns on the tip of the Skippers nose and potatoes warm the air. The beet smell dark red and Maud is setting the table.

Bessie comes in and starts to set up a small tray. She covers it with a cloth napkin and puts a special yellow china tea cup on the edge.

"I'll make his tea, Maud. He likes it a special way. And cut up all the food on his plate before it's brought to him. Put an extra napkin on the edge to tie around his neck and this china here is his special tea cup. He is the only one who's allowed to use it. You'll learn so don't be worried. You haven't set enough places."

"There's one fer you and one fer me. I had one set fer the Skipper but I can remove it."

"No, there should be one for me, and then one for my husband Earnest, another for Vince, that's his older brother, and one more for Arnold, the youngest of the Skipper's sons."

"What about me?"

"While we eat you can take your food up to your room and then return when we've finished supper...I still think of it as dinner, but here I suppose...when in Rome."

"You're from here?"

"Yes, but I've travelled. I've seen all the New England states and I've been over to Canada."

"I don't s'pose there'd be much travel for me in the job here?"

"From kitchen to parlour?"

They had their first laugh together and Maud noticed that Bessie even laughed different. She sounded like a good tea cup when you poured hot water in it. A delicate kind of gurgle. Maud tended to guffaw and slap at her thighs.

"Come up and I'll show you your room."

"Who owns the fiddle hung on the wall?"

"Ah, that's only Ern and his music. He'll drive you around the bend with his playing. Never stops it. Enough to give you a headache."

The steps creaked as they walked up and the cold was moving into the house. Away from the kitchen's fire and away from the parlour's Franklin stove you could feel the frost gripping the floorboards. It was coldest in the attic where the lamp showed Maud a slanting ceiling with wallpaper that was starting to bulge and that was torn in strips near one corner. The small cot she was to sleep in had galvanized tubing for a headboard, painted brown in the hope of giving it class. A porcelain basin and water jug stood in front of the window and an old dresser leaned against the wall with one side propped up by books that attempted to do the job of its missing leg.

"It's not really fixed up, Maud."

"Never mind that, if you got a hammer an' nails…"

"None of the boys will do it. They're too busy outside the house t'bother fixin' inside."

"I does that kind of thing meself. I was always handy and Father wasn't, so I does most everything."

"I'll leave you alone and call you when I've finished supper. You left your food in the kitchen."

"'Tis all right. I got t'get this packed away."

The room is hers, and tucked away in the attic of this house, it is far from the talk of her parents, far from the yells and demands of the younger children. She can hammer on another leg to the dresser an' out of her first ten dollars can do the wallpaper again. The dresser should go another colour. The brown would be painted yellow and the dresser too. As she stands and dreams, the cold is touching her until she starts to pace back and forth in the room. With quick hands she takes out woollen stockings, brown-ribbed and warm; her one good dress, blue with tiny white bows, and her three housedresses. A bandanna she got at the last garden party and her underdress made from faded flour sacks. She hangs her coat up in the dresser closet and looks once more around the room. Picking up the candle she can see her reflection in the window glass and is glad she braided up her hair instead of letting it ripple along her back.

"I looks more older, 'most twenty-one. The hair up gives me the looks I should have – not a little girl look – " She feels the knotted rise and runs her hand along the tight controlled hairdo. The fingers web out, like when she used to run them through the longness of her hair, but close again when she remembers that now she is controlled and a person of high position.

In her own room she hardly hears the faintness of Bessie's call, but when she does she moves as fast as a carried candle will allow her, and the little flame lights up the staircase like a sun.

"This," she thinks, "is gonna be a good place."

Chapter Two

It is quiet in George's Cove. When a dog does bark it's like a drip of water in a distant pail. Even the wind is rounded and blunts quietly against the stage head. The little boats are far away, their motors stopped as men check their nets. Kettles in kitchens are warming on the back of wood-burning stoves and when the children run out of doors they do so without a sound. Now their voices start and their feet tom-tom along the wharves. Amos Greenfield's schooner laps at the waves and the dogs shout to see children.

In galvanized tin pans warm water is mixing with yeast. The yellow and white Fleishmann's packages lie on wooden tables. Flour is being sifted and in other homes the frypan is melting fat-back pork. To the sounds that start to life the town, new smells are adrift all the way from the cove head to the stream where the young ones hold hands. Brewis that was soaking and fish that was stewing sizzle together in the big iron fry pots; tea changes smell from sharp to sweet, and tongue goes a-water as milk and sugar white up the cups. Bread is cut from foot high loaves and toast is burning in wire squares on the tops of stoves.

Where some had risen early, the Imp stove cleaner is blacking round the burners and sparkles like a steam engine. The kettles blur their shine onto a stove as clean as oil on cellophane.

Maud in her kitchen is looking out the window. She hears the first put-a-putta-putta-put, that is the sound of the one-lunger, the sound of the first of the boats coming back. The gulls hear it. From bobbing on the waves, from hanging round for a bit of garbage, they scream into the corners of the sky and wait for fish guts to hang down through the water.

The kettle whistles and Maud pours water on the tea leaves, then moves the small brown tea pot to the back of the stove. That used to be the Skipper's teapot. Not a delicate one like Bessie used. The ol' bugger was always mean.

"Steep the tea right this time, Maud, if you can. My God you are...Bessie, I said, My God, she be a clumsy girl."

"O hush now, Skipper," Bessie would say in that refined way she learned in Boston.

"Hush now, for she don't know no better. Don't clatter, Maud. Don't make as much racket."

Then the Skipper speaks again. "You knows how all I got left is ears. She knows that, Bessie. Them is me eyes now, Maud, you clumsy girl."

Bessie would come over and make the tea and, by God, the old man always knew she'd taken over. He'd smile and say, "Ern picked a proper girl to marry, Bessie. I hears in every sound how delicate you is. Maud, you watch her now and see the way 'tis done."

Then his fingers would climb up his grey frayed braces to the pocket in his red and black checked flannel shirt and would stub their way in until they pushed against the butt end of a plug of 'baccy.

"Where's me knife?"

"That old thing don't cut no more. I threw it away."

"Don't cut no more, Maud?" He almost cries. "I had that knife since I was a little boy. Me father gave that knife to me." He hears a step come near the kitchen.

"Ern, o Ern, she throwed away me knife" the one that Father give me." He sniffs.

Maud brushes past Ern, and Ern stands very, very still.

"Ern? Ern, I knows you'm there."

Now Maud's tea is steeped and she goes back to the window. The boats are nudging at the wharf and young Amador has tripped against the pilings. That young one is awful clumsy, thinks Maud. They all is now. 'Twas just that I was young when I started looking after the Skipper, an' he thought I was clumsy. 'Twas only that I were young.

First when Maud moved to George's Cove it was bigger. Now it had started to shrink. A lot of the young people had gone away to college or to vocational school and it seemed none of them ever came back. Sometimes at Christmas you'd see some young fella all dressed up and showing a new bride around the place. He'd be saying something and generally laughing, the woman taking great pleasure at wondering how so great a person had come from such humble beginnings. Now some of the houses were boarded over and the paint was beginning to peel on some of the first ones. Inside the boarded windows, it was like a series of small museums. None of the furniture removed or covered. Dishes left on kitchen shelves, old photos sepia-toned by time and now by dust. The old people of the house had died and the children were gone too far away to come back and pick over the possessions.

George's Cove, the Skipper had told her, was over two hundred years old. The man who'd founded it, George Hicks, had come over from Devonshire in England.

Sometimes when the storm blew sleet across the water, or when fog clung to lichen-licked rocks, or when the snow blew under a crack in the door, George cursed his hastiness in leaving England. But when the spring sun lifted scents from the moss and gentle winds helped dry the cod, or when he was in a boat looking back at the town he'd founded, George thanked God.

Chapter Three

This is Maud, and her legs are thick as cut beef and her hair is cheese-clothed to her head. She is forty, she is sitting on the edge of the feather bed, where it horseshoes her.

"My Jesus, 'tis cold."

Sing the song of an early morning stove, and you'll have to find rhymes for warm, and drift, and heat: the smell of hot iron. Sing the song of how the stove pushes warm air and the smell of hot water to the boil, and from bread the burn of, and the hiss and grease bubbles on the round of bologna. The molasses is dark and bitter from the night's dark dreams. Maud thinks of the mornings when she was little.

Polly put the kettle on
(When she was o so small)
Polly put the kettle on

The winter would be like a rough old board resting on her face. The winter would be a beach rock wrapped in cloth, a warm egg in the bed's buried feathers. How happy was a child's morning that pip of a grape of a day.

Now in the cooking her head is "O Polly put the kettle on," tilted to one side. The bread is always cut towards the breast. Thoughts scurry away, flash away from the thought of the breast cut.

The first time she saw Mother cut the bread, she'd turned her eyes away fast as a fish.

Maud takes her tea and goes to the rocker to drink it. Just like great grandmother. Grannie rocking by the stove, all the days of her life, and she would wind a small hankie round her hand and would pull tight first one finger, and then the other, and some would be wound across the stumps where her fingers used to be. They pale and even blue-veined and ever so white against the death of her husband. He of the strong shoulders, of the tight-across-the-shoulders suit too small for the pulpit beating, net-pulling shoulders. Oh they fade, they's gone – thinks Maud. His arms so strong, and the stories he would tell me. The white horse was a-gallop and all in blood from the death of his Master.

Great grandmother would sit by the stove. Every now and then, as soft as the move of a small mouse behind the stove, her voice would quiet into the warm.

"Poor me."

No one would listen. Father heaving in birch junks if special warm was needed. She was small, and playing with the kitten. Maud's legs brown-ribbed-in-long-stockings; legs so white where they met them like great grandmother's. Yes, she'd say "poor me" and Maud would ask why. Grannie would say, "What?" and Mother would laugh and Father would snort and move to the woodpile, letting the world winter a cold wind through the kitchen and a trail of snow would dust a white worm near the stove, and melt a thick line, dust still mixed with wet splinters of wood, near the wood box. And then great grandmother would nod and rock, and say to herself, "Poor me, poor me."

Once she told Maud, "I had a funny dream, and I still minds it. I were little and running towards father's stage. It was all sunny the day was, and there was a red woodshed nearby, and a circle painted on it to keep away the devil. The flakes were old, and high up like they were on top of a cliff..." Grannie interrupted herself. "Give me some dogberries."

Every fall, Maud would pick the dogberries, and would drop them into Grannie's white apron. She always wore in the day a small white apron over her black dress. "O, how I loved her" thought Maud. "And didn't even know it."

"How ugly you is, Grannie," Maud would say, and great grandmother would laugh and clap her hands and say "O goodie me, child, o goodie me."

When the dogberries came every year, Maud would pluck the berries, a lot if there was going to be a bad winter and scattered handfuls if there was going to be a good winter. She'd pass over the bitter wood-tasting berries to the old woman who would cup in her tiny stubbed hand the berries and would slowly chew them. Maud would pretend to like the dogberries and eat a few and all her nose could smell was the bitter green of the sap on the edge of the bark and great grandmother would smile at her, munch the berries, or would hold them in her mouth until they must have been a tree again and she'd say, "Good for the blood." Grannie ate more dogberries, and returned to the tale of her dream.

"But Maud, I'd be running and then I tripped and crashed through the flakes, and tumbled head-over-kettles down to the sea. So strange. And my child, I remember that better than real things."

Maud dreamed about flying and wet her bed. The feathers smelled and she was whipped, still she dreamed the same dream but was too small to talk about it. It was a secret.

Great grandmother had a small book and Maud would read stories from the book, and great grandmother would sleep.

Great grandmother was called Irene and she grew up in an outport near St. John's. She grew up in a small white house, with a big yard of hay, of grass and some flowers at the right time of year.

The windows were white water clear in tone but a border of coloured glass ran round them, rectangles of green, rectangles of red, blue and silver, and o how the world looked first all green, and then in a sideways-flash it went green-blue-silver-yellow and all the world was like looking through a bottle. She would stand there by the hour till when she turned back inside the house it was all a-ring with colour, like coming out of a faint. It would carry a green cast and her mother's apron would look green. She'd dream of being able to take the window with her wherever she travelled so the world could be what she wanted it to be.

All the kitchen ceiling was done in boards like the floor and was painted white. The walls were covered with wall covering that each year grew thicker until it was at last stopped and painted white. The big horse was grey. There were geese that scattered and blew their noses and hissed and scared her, and there was the smell that jumped from the pigpen, and the caplin on the beach that was another time of year smell, and the lobster tossed on the compost heap that as it salted into decay was another scent to tickle the nose. The richest and blackest smell was the tarring of the roof, and the look of it and the odour...stiff brushes moving against the hot tar then stopped hot to the sun and shinning like a stove top. Father in wostered socks walking backward and spreading tar.

"O" said great grandmother, "Mother would call us all to dinner, and we had to wait till father said the blessing, and we would eat. Hard to hold the knife, it slips in the hand and is too big, like the fork – a grown-up trying to eat with a pitchfork."

Now Maud looks out the window and all the voices from the past fade. Because she sees Ern walking by and all the sky is around him like he was carrying it on his back.

Chapter Four

Maud plays the tin whistle as she walks to the dance.

> *O the Billy goat chased*
> *The Nanny goat*
> *Over the fields and*
> *tore her*
> *Petticoat.*

The moon shining on the whistle glints blue at Maud and she does a little side step, feeling the gravel roll and hearing it crunch under her shoes.

"Ern always forgets. He'd forget me if I didn't tag along."

O the Billy goat...

Stopping for a minute, Maud listens to the boats creak against the wharf.

The moon lights Ern's boat bobbing at the mooring dipping on the waves and nodding into the wind. Maud smells fish in the breeze and the tar on the fishing nets still fresh from this morning. She and Ern, the pot bubbling over a pile of driftwood and the smell just like the way it looked – all black bubbles and light skim. Now the smell still clinging to the edge of her nostrils, stronger than the fish, darker than the night.

Sound leaks out of the Orange Lodge. When small, she would hear the name and think they made the Christmas oranges there. One night she asked her father to bring an orange back home. O, how he laughed and then told Uncle Dick and poor Mother and they all laughed. She, a little girl in the middle of the kitchen with no place to go, feeling the woollen stockings band her scrawny legs, her cotton dress hold her in the middle of the room with everyone laughing and Father saying –

"O, that's a good one. My sweet Jesus, that's a good one. Wait 'til I tell the b'ys."

Poor Mother laughed and said, "Now I knows what them old initiation rites is…all you fools picks the Christmas oranges.

That stopped Father's laughs for, as Maud found out later in her life, the Orange Lodge was not to be laughed at, like true religion and God, really for men only.

Now forty years later and in another place, a different Orange Lodge rolls the music out the door and other men line the railing outside its porch. Moonlight not only glints from the tin whistle, it shines off bottles. The men have shirt sleeves rolled up and their backs steam like horses in the early morning.

Inside she hears the sound of Ern playing the accordion. She doesn't need to see to know it's him. Maud knows the way he plays anything and let it be tin whistle, guitar, accordion or the painted bottles, she can still hear Ern through his music the same way she could see him from the way his nets were wove.

Coming through the door she sees the Time in full swing. Aladdin lamps hanging from the ceiling move circles around the dancers swirling through Sevens & Eights. Ern's foot taps and he heaves back on the accordion. Sweat trickles into his eyes and they blink like mice coming into the light.

"My God, how his bald spot sends the light back. 'Tis getting' bigger, but I s'pose I better not tell him. Funny the way men combs they foolish little hairs…"

Ern's foot taps and taps and his pant leg rides up showing the red socks Maud knit him.

"O my Jesus, Maud, you don't expect me t'wear them things. Everyone else got grey socks. Me mother always knitted grey ones. Whoever heard of red socks?"

They look very fine, thinks Maud. Bit of life to them and when they were hung out on a line the Monday air brightened right up. Next to the bloomers she hung them. By God, that made them look embarrassed when she caught people starin'. O Ern kicked up 'bout wearin' them, but she knew that inside he smiled and chuckled, laughed away. He couldn't fool her…never could.

Down goes the accordion and Ern whips a saw out from under his straight-back chair. The chair with the white paint flaking off showing where it used to be green, just a few years after it was red.

Maud stops and looks up at Ern. He winks and tilts his head, nods at a place on the floor where she lays the whistle as he's slipping a notched wooden handle over the top of the saw's blade.

"This is the way you plays the saw, Maud," he told her when she first knew him. "Just put the handle over the top of the blade, now bend her to the left or right – don't matter – 'til she's all crooked one way, then buckle back the top part – no, t'other way, so she's like an 'S'. Now hit her with this mallet an' shake it a little."

The blade sang a note that moved into her wrist and up her arm while her ear sent a thrill down to her shoulders. O, the quiver and the sing of it…that sweet, sweet sound. Like the start of a tickle. Now she hears him flow the notes into each other as the saw buckles and catches the reflections from people.

Maud shakes her head and stares towards the back of the hall.

Unpainted wooden benches line the long sides and on the left, the young men sit – on the right the young women. The husbands of older women are smoking and yarning down in one corner and they talk low, long, and laugh a lot. Most of the younger men are out on the rail, the more timid ones coming back in quickly. Two small boys have pulled the wings off a fly and are trying to make it go the way they want it to by prodding its side with old match sticks.

Maud hesitates and moves through the swirling dancers. She picks up the beat of the song and almost dances through the middle of the dance floor, round this couple and then round another. If some other woman had done this everyone would have smiled, but not for Maud. They just look at her and away quickly. Maud wears a polka dot bandanna made out of Ern's hankies tied around her head and she wears a blue house dress. Her shawl's like a crazy quilt. Stopping – Maud shakes out her hair and the black rush of it curls down her back and bounces back.

"Thank God there's Sue to talk with…" she smiles. "Sue, how's she goin', ol girl? Where you been?"

Sue pauses a moment and smiles her approval for the shawl. "Where *you* been is more like it. You'm the one comin' in late."

"Ern forgot the whistle again...Every dance 'tis the same."

"I was over to see Aunt Sadie Green. She don't look too good, Maud."

"She never did look too good."

"Now, Maud! Speak kindly of the dead."

"When she is. You got any cheerful news?"

"I remember that look in poor Harry's eyes...they clouded over and the lids got bitter."

"You calls that cheerful news?"

"You must be awful sick of goin' back t'fetch that whistle."

"Well, Sue, you know how 'tis – like they said about Uncle George Tilley, the only reason he lived so long was 'cause he was too absent-minded to die when he got old."

The music stops jigging and slowly it begins to spin again, this time as a waltz. People are clapping and now Ern looks at Maud before he starts playing. Her arms look strong and pale. Ern, looking over the heads of the dancing people, is reminded of the first time he saw her bare arm. She was dusting that dresser that he and Bessie were given on their wedding day. Maud's sleeve fell back and a younger even fairer arm slid up towards the bureau top. Ern wanted to touch her arm, to kiss it, lick it. Instead he went downstairs to talk with Bessie, a wife he couldn't like no matter how he tried.

Ern is moving through the dancers and, the same as Maud, he moves in time to the music. Maud starts to move towards him and they dance before they meet.

A grand bow does Ern make to Maud and they dance through the people alone. From the benches she can hear gossip floating up as they drift past the room's edges.

"Ern might listen..."

"Maud might think..."

"So long together now they might as well be..."

"But they aren't..."

"She can play a tune as good as Ern..."

"O, he might listen t'her play a tune."

"...but he wouldn't marry her. She ain't the kind you'd...marry. No, she got a sight too much lip..."

Now they dance in the room's centre and all they hear is the music, all they see is the spin of the other dancers. Ern always pretends not to hear the gossip and, as Maud gets angrier and angrier, he dances suppleness back to her, lives the sway of the music and then the voices stop their echo in her head and they are close together. From the rafters you would see Maud and Ern in the exact centre of the dance, waltzing around the hub of the waltz. You would see Ern, a little circle of a man, hold the square-cut Maud, hold this block of a woman and they together spin and turn, whirl and waltz as one – both the circle and the square.

When the music stops, Ern goes back to his accordion and Maud sits with Sue. This time neither of them talks and Maud's strong fingers dance red wool on needles and click, click as Maud and Sue sit and watch the dance.

Chapter Five

The kitchen is yellow-tiled halfway up the walls, then a white enamel carries up to the ceiling. Although the same colour paint is used on the ceiling, it looks different because of the boards that run slantwise and start to buckle near the edges. Both Maud and Ern are short people and it's as if the house were designed for them. Anyone over five foot five hits their head on the ceiling and even Maud and Ern have to duck when going through some doorways.

Bessie never felt easy here and was always seen rubbing her head. Maud, on the other hand, could always stand straight and proud, the top of her head just brushing the ceiling.

There's a black stove with cream trim that can burn either wood or coal, and next to it a roughly fashioned green wood box which always contains half a cord of wood and fifty million spiders. The warmer on top of the stove has socks across its open door and in the oven Maud is drying out some kindling that got wet last night. The smell of heating wood drifts up with the odour of bologna singeing in a pan. There's a clothes line running from the top of the stove to a nail in the wall and on the line more of Ern's red socks are drying. There's a paint-by-number of The Last Supper on one wall with Christ seeming to stare out of the frame. That happened because the Skipper called out for Maud just as Bessie was painting the Saviour's eye with number fifteen blue. He called so loud that the eye now peered at a flight of plaster ducks ascending the wall. There was an extra detail of authenticity to the ducks for two wings had been knocked off and there was a spattering of plaster shrapnel across their bellies. Maud had thrown a plate at Ern once and hit the ducks instead.

On the wall where the porch door comes into the kitchen hangs a bamboo framed "Bless This House." It is done with glitter paint on a black sheet of paper and over the years the damp has carried off the "B" and part of the "H."

On a shelf on the daybed wall there's a brown bakelite radio atop the red and blue of an Eveready battery, with its black cat jumping away from the sparks. And under the radio, asleep on the black leather daybed, lies Ern. He's snoring with his mouth open and when he shifts his head Maud can see the imprint made across Ern's cheek. One boot is on, one suspender strap is off, and his shirt is unbuttoned. Around the edge of the Stanfield's undershirt Maud can see that a fringe of grey hairs is a-tangle. Just after it seemed he was goin' bald the few poor hairs he had left all went grey.

Maud hesitates for a moment and then she picks up a hammer from the finished cupboards she's been building in the kitchen. She gives a protruding nail a mighty smack and one of Ern's eyes slowly opens.

"Breakfast is ready, my son. I got some bologna fried." Ern's reaction is bilious. "And some strong tea."

Ern's expression calms and half a smile begins. He looks at a hook in the wall to make sure his fiddle is hung up the proper way. It is.

Legend has it that even when Ern passes out after a night of playing, just before he hits the floor there's one thing he always does. He folds his hands around the fiddle and turns to face the wall so he's sure to fall on his back and never hurt the fiddle.

"What time is it?"

"Time enough t'be up. 'Tis a fine day fer a change, so you better get goin' and finish the trim round the front of the house. Have some exercise. God knows you needs it. I got to make some bread and finish them cupboards."

By this time Ern is sitting up and aware that he's already almost dressed for the morning. He pulls on his left boot, loops a suspender over his shoulder and begins to button his shirt.

'By God, that saves a lot of time in the morning."

"What?"

"Goin' t'bed half dressed. No – don't bother with the grub, put it in th' warmer till I comes back in."

Maud shrugs. "All right, Ern, I got too much work t'do t'stand round an' watch you eat."

She puts the bologna on a rippled plate edged with faded blue, known as the 'Seagull' pattern when it flew in the middle of packages of soap flakes. The plate is put in the warmer after Ern's socks have been pinned to the line with wooden clothes pins. The clothes are damp and rough to the fingers.

Maud picks up a hammer and starts the cupboards.

"Fer God's sake, me poor head."

"Well, b'y, I got to get them finished fer me precious china. I needs the shelves fer that o so dainty shavin' mug y'won't let me throw out and perhaps fer your ol' pisspot. But if I'm disturbin' your majesty I'll begin me bread again."

She picks up a large earthenware bowl, the outside the colour of dried egg yolk, the inside the colour of fried egg white. Inside the bowl Maud pours warmed milk and the little globes of Fleischmann's yeast. Her mother used to use liquid – kept it in that grouty lookin' ol' bottle in the kitchen. Father used it to start his brews, too, an' always when he was drunk he'd tease Maud by bringing her close to him and there, with his hands gripping her so she could never get loose, he would stare her in the eyes and breathe alcohol all over her face. All the men in the kitchen would laugh and she had nowhere to hide.

"Listen, Maud," he'd breathe, "how'd you like a nice slice of bread?"

She'd shake her head. "No, I got to go to bed now."

Her father would grin. "Does you, my child. Well, what you needs is a good slice of bread. Not the kind your mother makes but what I bakes in that ol' barrel."

O the men would laugh and Father would release his grip but she'd walk ever so slowly, backwards towards the hall door, scared that if she ran he'd grab her again.

"Yes, we both uses the same yeast but the by's likes eatin' mine a whole lot better."

Upstairs in bed she'd reach her feet down under the covers and rest them on the towel around the stones that Mother had heated for her bed. Then she'd wish that the heat were all over the bed instead of just where her feet were. Maud always wanted to reach down for the bricks but she knew if she made that grab the cold air would pour down her shoulders like water and then all through the bed. The moonlight blued the slanted wall and through the thin door she could hear her mother stirring in her sleep and the sound of the fog horn over the invisible water...Oooo-wah...Ooooooo-wah...Ooooooo waaaaaaaha... mourning at the shore. The chill was going away from everywhere but her face. O so cold it was in the run into your nightdress, the cold air scraping everywhere, and the quick hunching over the pisspot – "No," Mommy said, "don't call it that, call it chamber pot." "Chamber piss pot," would laugh Father. Whatever you called it, when she made her water she could hear it tinkle on the ice and then hiss down through. The morning would be colder. Now the sleepy wallpaper would buckle and she could hear bursts of laughter come up the stairs. She'd sleep in laughter and perhaps wake up later when her father would crash up the step and try to wake up her mother, and the feather bed would rock against the floor and her mother cry and cry until her father swore his way into sleep and she'd follow.

Back in their kitchen Ern has picked up his tin whistle and starts to play on it an air he played for Maud after the first time they slept together. He pauses and she looks over at him from across the kitchen table. He plays it again, softer and slower than the first time he played it. For as each year of their being together passes by, the tune changes as well. Always the same notes in the same order but with alterations in the tone, the pauses and the breathing. Now so soft was it that Maud almost drifted away from the bread bowl and Ern's face took on the old look.

"No, me son, much as I'd like to, we got bread started and you got that painting to do, so stop that playin' before I makes a fool of me, an' you. Besides, think of what that thrashin' around 'ud do t'your head."

"Ern grimaces. "You're right, Maud...this morning. This afternoon you'll be wrong."

"I knows that. We got plenty of time. Go do your paintin', an' leave the whistle out. I wants to try an' play an air meself this afternoon. Go 'way now, b'y, 'cause I'll never get any work done."

The fish are being unloaded and the younger men are using pitchforks to toss the cod up on the wharf. Some fish still squirm. Small boys run round until they are ordered away. Older boys know the way of the wharf and stand quietly watching every move. Knives are being sharpened. Wooden buckets are made ready, their ropes uncoiled.

Ern pries up the lid and drives the stirring stick through the skin that covers the red paint. A gush of oil makes his nostrils rabbit and he sniffs. The outside of the house has been painted a new shade of white, covering up the old buff colour and, in the sunlight, it sparkles as if the nails were silver and driven with a pewter hammer. Alone on a hill it stands, the prettiest little house in George's Cove. "Like a nipple on a tit," thinks Ern. The land slopes away in all directions and the fence around the property makes a perfect circle. It is painted white. A walk has been made to the front door, covered in gravel and sea shells and lined on either side by beachrocks. Once, after they'd whitewashed the fence, Maud kept using the brush in a burst of fun and whitewashed every rock on the property. Now they no longer use whitewash on the fence but they still whiten the rocks every spring and it always looks to Ern like Maud put hankies out to dry all over his land. The Skipper, despite his faults, had picked good land, the best. Ern finishes stirring the paint and now he moves towards the scaffold left by the front of the house.

On the wharf all the fish have been landed and now the gutting starts. From back to front the knives slit, opening the silver belly showing red and yellow-blue glints. The guts are hauled out in one handful and flung to float on water until the gulls claw downward. The blood runs along wooden splitting tables, scarred with knife marks and rounded with age. The planked buckets are lowered and at the last second a flip of the wrist tilts the bucket so it will fill with water. The water from the sea washes blood and strings of gut back into itself and the splitting continues. More blood runs on the wood.

Ern's brush dips in the red paint and lifts to the eaves. In the middle of the motion his face suddenly squinches up and he grabs at his chest with both hands, the paint going red across his shirt. His neck tendons up and like wire coat hangers his muscles strain. In a reel sideways he sees a red filter between him and the sun. In great surprise, he sees that through the pain he can look right into the sun and it won't hurt his eyes.

And in the sun is a dance and now in the middle of the pounding in his ears, he hears, played slower than ever, the song he made for Maud. All the light is sun and nothing hurts his eyes.

A small boy on the stage head looks up towards the house and having just learned the quietness of the wharf, says nothing as he sees Ern pause in the middle of a brush stroke. He sees the spin towards him.

Amador Major looks at where young Kevin is staring and sees Ern fall. Ern doesn't fall away from the house. He thuds inside the web of scaffold and is bounced with his paint can along the clapboard, and Amador sees red spill down the house's white. Ern lies there with red paint on his shirt front and dripping down his head.

The crash reaches Maud as, hands in dough and flour, she moves towards the table's centre to knead the dough to final form. She rushes out the door and can hardly lift the latch with boxing gloves of bread upon her hands. Red, the knuckles strain and now the dough is spread upon the door and flour puffs in the breeze that through the kitchen door is blowing.

"Ern, Ern, Ern, me lovely."

Cradled in her arms, paint is smeared onto her apron to mix with flour and yeast. His head is powdered with her hands as she strokes and croons and wonders.

When they reach the scene the men are solemn and three of them, Amador Major, Obadiah Neil and Victor Maynard, carry Ern towards the kitchen.

No one comforts Maud, though some move closer, and everything is silent. The boy sees the paint and flour and starts to giggle, then to laugh.

Ern is brought into the kitchen, is put on the daybed and they loosen up his shirt.

But it is no use – no use at all.

For Ern is dead.

Chapter Six

Salted fish are drying on the flakes. On top of blasty boughs they rest and salt is whitening to the sun. The older men can tell you who put up the fish as surely as if everyone had signed each open fish. The women wear long black dresses and white aprons. From the distance they look like crows picking over dry bleached bones. They move back and forth turning over fish so the sun can dry each side. The boughs crack and rattle under their feet and the old wood of the stage makes creaking sounds. They gather the fish into threes when it looks done and build them into stacks. Then the tarpaulin is placed over the fish. Today is a grey one and there's a taste of damp and salt in the air. The sky darkens while clouds shift slowly.

See Mabel Squires, her face as smooth as if it had been sandpapered and cheeks red to the wind. White hairs escape from her bonnet and wisp her face. She doesn't bother to brush them back but every now and then bites off one that tickles her lip.

"What do you s'pose Maud's gonna do?"

"Do? Only one thing to do an' that's t'go home," Cavelle answers, and her angles are all fish bones next to the roundness of Aunt Mabel. She knew what Maud should do, just as she'd always known the correct behaviour for anyone in the cove at all times. "She's got t'go back to her people, back to her real home, where she were born."

"Cavelle, my dear…she been with Ern twenty years."

"No difference. Family is family, an' property is property."

"They never forgave her, I 'low."

"Still, blood is blood."

As Cavelle talks, her thinness feels the damp move closer to the bones, feels the water hung in the sky just waiting for the proper shake of wind, and she hurries.

All over the flakes the women are hurrying and rushing back and forth. Tarpaulins are flung with strong hands, with sure hands; tarred ropes are quickly tied and fish is hidden from the wind, salt is hidden from the damp's lick. Inside the sailcloth the smell is hanging warmed back on itself. Only boughs are left to blow and rattle their needles in the wind. Round twigs will catch the drops in wooden creases. The fish is all secure, the church bell is ringing in the damp, counterpointing the foghorn. It peals between the movings of the women, it sentences out their talk and breathes the pauses in their gossip.

"When you was speakin' to Ern you never knowed how t'mention Maud."

The bell is clanging on the short pipe length that holds it 'cross the steeple and old hands are tugging at the rope. It sways through grey and tings at the first rain drops that run along its lip.

"You couldn't ask Ern, 'How's the Missus?' 'Cause he'd have to say 'dead'. Bessie of course, God rest her soul. God rest..."

The bell clangs out and pauses at the bell ringer wipes his forehead with an old blue dotted hankie.

"...God rest his soul."

"Vince be comin' back to claim what's his be rights."

"Maud sent him an' Arnold telegrams. They'll be home."

"Mightn't come, maid."

"No, no. They bound to. Vince got t'come back an' settle things."

The bell was cheap and its tone was never very full but the flatness of the note carried farther in the cove than the roundness of a full one. It scraped your ears, it spoke of death and of the grave. It sounded like a shovel in the grit and grated like brown paper on wet soaked fingers. When the bell called you into church it called you into the graveyard.

"Won't be long now."

Black skirts brush against tarpaulins and sweep the needles off the branches down through the stage onto the rats' backs. They scurry, swish tails and speed down burrows as the rain and needles rattle fright that carries underground. The smell of fish drifts down the tunnels; it crusts along the rats' nest as the footsteps stop the shaking of the posts. Rats slide out and listen to the stillness that moves to fill in where the bell pauses. All that's heard are voices drifting along the footpath and wrapped up in the fog.

"Arnold's back too?"

"You knows Arnold. He'd follow Vince anywhere."

"S'pose Maud wants t'keep the house? Not give it to the brothers?"

"She might."

"No chance, maid, no chance."

Looking down at the cover, before the clouds roll over to spoil our view, you can see by the wharf near Ern's house a small boat. The engine cuts, fog swallows the echoes, its prow hits a rubber tire hung on the pilings. Suitcases are piled round the two men who reach for the wharf. The footpath is empty except for one old man who's walking towards the water.

Ern's house now stands alone and if you were to walk around it, your steps would bury in the grass until the crunch of gravel when you reached the path. The thin smoke of a well-banked fire is drifting out of the stovepipe and all the blinds are drawn in the windows. The front door is left ajar despite the damp and in the kitchen Sue is making tea.

The house has no more scaffold but red paint still bleeds the front. Other houses have blinds up and they scatter colours around the cove mouth. One small bungalow is half orange, half white and, in one corner, the greens and browns predominate; there the reds hold forth. And square biscuit box, they corner colour at the air and most are as clean as if the sea had washed them. Waves wash garbage back towards the shore and in the water near a small group of homes, the rusty parts of motors are hooking kelp and letting the seaweed grow through pinwheels.

The stores are closed and over to the far side of the cove, across the hill where the other footpath winds, round the stream and along a cliff, over to a meadow near the church, where the graveyard holds the people of the town, and damps the children into quiet. The tombstones are simple and over some small mounds the crosses of white wood are rusting stains from old nails.

The bell stops and she walks to the door and closes it. Inside, the kitchen warms and Sue pours herself a cup of tea. She wonders what she'll say to Maud, sipping the tea until it almost burns her lip. Her eyes look at the fiddle hanging on the wall and then to the Last Supper.

Chapter Seven

Feet are splashing waves in puddles and mud stirs up clouds coffee-brown in their centres. Boots are soaked and trouser cuffs get wet and cling to ankles. The grave is wet around the edges. Every now and then a clump of earth sighs down into the hole. Small rocks roll down the sides and splash into an inch of water in the bottom. Most of George's Cove stands in the small graveyard at the church front. Children play near the toolshed that house the shovels and the picks. Fathers are looking uncomfortable in blue serge suits and mothers are wearing shawls or sombre bandannas. One of the pallbearers is taller than the rest and muttered comments about the swaying of the casket make him turn red. Amador and Obadiah wear white shirts with black ties and have on their navy windbreakers. In their lapels are mourning ribbons and around their arms the black bands.

The service starts and all have bowed their heads but still sneak looks at Maud. Most had bet she wouldn't be there.

"Shockin' the way she didn't go near the casket at his wake – an' he done up so pretty."

" 'Twas a good thing that Uncle Elias' son, Tom, were home."

He was an undertaker near Deer Lake and having Ern die while he was there was a good way for him to show off his skill. He'd improvised with his wife's makeup and some cotton bought from Billy Joe Simmonds' grocery store. And some extra rouge had helped put the natural look back in Ern. It was a great source of professional pride the way the local people had praised up Ern. One little old lady saying he hadn't looked as good since he was twenty. The only disappointment was Maud's lack of interest. He gained comfort when he thought she wasn't really a widow. When Tom went into St. John's at the annual meeting he must tell people how good a job you can do with only limited equipment. Maybe even a paper for the Undertaker's Digest. Now he grimaces as the pallbearers almost drop the dearly beloved.

Maud has not dressed properly. In the midst of mud and mud-shade colours her dress blazes its electric blue and her sweater as white as whitewashed beachrocks is certainly wrong. She stands solid with her chin still up and her eyes staring straight ahead.

"I tells you," whispers Mrs. Squires to Cavelle, "I wept more in one minute than she'm wept in three days."

Maud's face suddenly stiffens and she looks for the first time in the direction of the casket. Mrs. Squires sees the change in her face and feels quite content until she notices other people's faces brightening up. At least, lighting up as much as one is allowed to at a funeral. She follows the direction of their gaze and sees behind the toolshed, and coming up the hill, Vince and Arnold. Vince looks even more handsome and seems, though he's still in the distance, to wear a rich overcoat. Arnold, who carries two suitcases, is fatter than he ever was and looks short next to Vince. Vince walks stilt-like in wide strides. Arnold walks like he still has tin-can-horses on his feet. Maud looks at them again and her face stays tight.

The words of the service are muted as they splash across the field to the two brothers. Vince looks along the row of mourners and laughs.

"Jesus, Vince, this is no place t'laugh."

"They can't hear a word we say, Arnold, they'll think we're braving up to get by graveside. I was laughing 'cause it was so easy t'spot Maud. I'd have thought they changed her. Still different, look at that dress... I'm glad we're here to see it."

Arnold rests and the suitcases are sinking in the mud. He notices but is too tired to care. Vince is talking again anyway – "My God, don't he ever shut up," thinks Arnold.

"Hell of a way to have to come home, Arnold, but it's still good to get here. Nothing's changed. Only thing bigger is the graveyard."

"The place is smaller." Arnold looks at the fresh grave. "We should have made the wake."

"Ern's not gonna care. He won't kick up no fuss. Maud's the one who's gonna wish we stayed away."

"I don't think it's the time to bring up that house thing."

Ern's casket is being lowered into the grave and the ropes are slippery with the mud that browns along their length. Near the end the coffin tilts down faster on the front and splashes in the growing water in the grave.

Vince shakes his head.

The fishermen walk toward the hole where the casket is lying and each breaks a wooden gaff across his knee. When the wood parts they throw the broken pieces in on top of the coffin and then the dirt starts showering, rattling and then sticking to the wooden lid.

Pastor Roberts has finished his work and normally he'd move over to comfort the wife. Seeing as Maud is the only thing close to a wife and she doesn't really count, he moves towards the family. He is grateful to Vince and Arnold because it might have looked a little harsh otherwise if he'd ignored Maud.

"Hello, hello, hello, Vince. Welcome home. Back to stay?"

"No, Pastor, it's just a visit."

"I knew Arnold's was."

Maud stands by herself looking across the cove towards the house. In her mind she is listening to the start of Ern's song. It begins slow.

The sound of wet gravel being thrown gives a slap-slap beat to the music, and the grey of the sky begins to lighten.

She thinks back to that time just after the Skipper's funeral, and she and Ern were alone in the house. All the blinds were down, and "just as well," said Ern to Maud," 'tis bad enough what they think we do, if they could see us they'd really get ready t'throw you out of town. Maud. I'd marry you..."

"No need to, b'y. I don't believe in it much. Me mother and father went to the church an' done it proper and I can still hear her cryin' in the night. No, Ern, I wants t'keep me independence. If ever the day comes when 'tis over, I don't want it t'be like you an'..."

"Bessie? 'Sides it's nice t'spite them ol' gossips and that clergyman. 'Ern,' he says t'me, 'now that your father's dead, 'tis time fer Maud to pack her things and get out of your house.' "

Ern walked from the bed and pulled up the blind. The sun rolled over his naked body and lit his roundness. Maud looked down at her flat hard belly and saw the sun spill angles on it.

"Ern, me son, come back from the window."

Without pulling down the blind he walked back, and from the dresser drawer took out a tin whistle. He sat down and started a run on the whistle. It changed from a run to a pattern, then somehow the sunlight, the way the blankets were rumpled and the shadows on his crotch, the light on hers all started to become notes in the song he was playing. High and then low, slow and then fast and their life together in the pouring of the notes. The music brought back Bessie, poor mad Bessie, at the end of her life when she thought she was the Queen. The Skipper would grope his way into the song and then, growing younger, his eyes would light up again and the waves rolled over teeming cod inside his pupils when he danced round a kitchen with Ern held in his arms. Then Maud noticed her arms made bare as her sleeves rolled back, and all so quiet the whistle ran the quietness of the crack of the stove while she saw Ern look through Bessie to her arms.

And then the song ended. Yet it didn't and as they lay and moved through wet together and slowly rolled against each other. Maud looked down at Ern, his hips rising off the bed, and then they rolled together on their sides, the song kept singing and part of it was knowing the blind was up, and the world's sky was looking.

Now the song has stopped and all that's left is the final splash with the rattle of rocks when mud is upon the casket's mound. And all that's left is Maud watching the gravediggers finish, and all that's left are Arnold and Vince talking to the Pastor.

"Ern, O Ern, he didn't speak, the man of the cut cloth, the two dollar bible gilted round the cover, and the red words for Jesus didn't talk to me."

From behind it's Vince calling out to Maud and the sound of his voice as if he'd never left; the same age to it, same sound as the first time she'd heard it. She still remembered the way he had looked at her, staring at her, the new girl come to work in the Skipper's house.

Now his footsteps are upon the wet grass.

"Hello Maud."

They close together and Vince is by her. He moves and he is ahead of her, has shifted into the side-step around her like when in the kitchen he walked around her to taste of the soup she was making, that with the smell of tinned tomatoes, of fresh cabbage the smell drifting as quick as fast as Vince in his sock feet, never the move to touch, but the sly look, and the move towards Maud then.

"I said hello, Maud."

"A surprise, Vince, t'see you here. That you'd fly down at all from as far away as that Toronto, I thought 'twas too big t'fly across let alone out of it."

Vince stops and laughs. The sound of the foghorn is in between his breaths and his laughs. He looks around as Maud keeps walking and feels the wet of his feet, his socks damp and steaming from the wool-heat.

The path is narrow, and Maud's back seems to fill it, as she walks away, as her steps move from the stamp of wet grass and moss to the crunch and she's away leaving a dent in the air. She leaves. Even the sound of her feet has gone away, and Vince is old and tired with his watching.

Chapter Eight

I t's in Billy Joe Simmonds' store.

And there they are, Vince and Arnold by the round rough iron stove where the heat is almost too much for the morning, but chairs are drawn up, and crates have edged near like there's a winter frost about an inch from the back of every man. The clergyman is poking at the coals with the burnt end of a stick and at the counter Billy Joe is spinning off a bit of twine from the ball that is rounding near the ceiling. The string leads through an eye-holed screw and back to Billy Joe. He holds down a sheet of brown paper over salt beef, and as it stains the paper, he ties the string and reaches for the cash register, pauses, and in pencil begins to write the figures on to the scribbler paper bill of sale...one pound of salt beef, and licks the pencil tip, whittled to a roundness by his large old pocket knife with the half of the handle fallen off.

Silly Fred is sweeping up, a foolish grin as he watches the Dustbane mountain roll in little green boulders over the floor. He wants to lie down and play roads, and run his fingers through and have a good smell of the Dustbane but he'll get a clout from the old man, so he just leans so he's almost tipping as he sweeps.

"Vince, my son, it's good to have you back. The church is still standin' as good as ever, and I hope your voice is as good as it was. But, of course, the roof needs shingles, tho' God's got a clear view."

It's quiet and they wait to see if Pastor Roberts wants an answer, or if he's ready to preach a sermon at them. It stays quiet, and all the stove people hear is the sweep of the broom. They glance at Fred.

Arnold has got a bit of kindling and he's whittling it into a circle of strands like a birch broom. He's not even looking up. Look real close and you can see that he's happy, so happy it hasn't got a lot to do with what anyone is saying, or where he is. It's hooked up with the whittling, the way the knife feels against his hand, the way – where his hands are soft now – that it's beginning to hurt a little. His head is massive and held tilt to his shoulder line. His glasses are thick, have black rims, and some scotch tape is holding the arm to the frame. He's smiling and smelling the wood, and, at the edge of his nose, the Dustbane, which makes him think of school. And that thought drifts by.

Pastor Roberts is wondering if he should have said the church is still in good shape. 'Cause Vince looks like he might have a little money, maybe a lot, and there were things to be done.

You haven't seen much of Amador or Obadiah yet, and you usually wouldn't. They are right here, but have learned how to hang back a bit and listen before they talk a lot. Amador thinks quick but he likes to cover that up by seeming to take a while to hear and then figure out what's going on. He has a narrow face with a soft mouth and a light chin. He usually lets a couple of days' whiskers hang on his face to take the edge off. He likes the women and has a small bottle, tiny and pink, called 'Talk' and when he's with a woman, he'll put a drop on his tongue to make his breath smell nice. He goes to the movies every Wednesday and Friday night, and hopes there's a cowboy movie on so he can think that he's got the guitar, and sings to the pretty schoolteacher. Amador has a real guitar at home, but it only cost seven dollars in the catalogue and is smaller than he thought it was going to be, and has a palm tree on it and a dancing girl. Mostly Amador plays the guitar alone in his room and he lets his cigarette hang low on his lip and he sees the smoke curl from a long way away like he was watchin' himself in the movies. He's looking at Vince right now and thinking that Vince looks something like Victor Jory, and Arnold looks like Smiley Burnett with big thick glasses.

Obadiah is thinking that Vince is looking rich, dressed real fine, and he's a bit embarrassed that the pastor is starting to hint about money, but that's what the message comes to after all the shuffling and the hand clinging. Like they forgot everything and took a little tug to the side with a cod jigger, and tried to catch up a bit of money.

On the outside, Billy Joe's store is grey, painted new and fresh so as to make grey look like an interesting colour. The shingles are Cape Cod size, and a large hand-painted sign is done in green on fresh white. "Billy Joe Simmonds" and underneath, "Groc. And Conf." It's got a veranda like a platform leading up to the door, and is built across two rocks and it's there that Fred pushes the wheelbarrow full of groceries for home delivery. Whenever he sees someone looking, he comes to a dead stop, puts down the barrow, and tilts back his hat and gives a big smile, until you'd look somewhere else, then he'd be on his way.

Inside, the talk is starting, and Vince talks slow and strong like a Nova Scotia salesman who's trying to talk and remember the kids' names all at the same time. He talks of the city, of Toronto, and makes it sound like a far off place of magic. Pastor Roberts is smiling and looks confident, like he'd been the one who coaxed Vince into talking about this city.

Amador is looking at Vince and wondering how many movie houses a city could have. And still Vince goes on. He finds his strength in the quiet of those listening, in the creak of the stove as the heat expands the iron, in the way the pastor is doing a light clearing of his throat, keeping the motor turning over. Arnold still whittles, because he lives in Toronto and doesn't need the stories.

"Got myself a little house, and then a bigger. O, must be as many people as are in all George's Cove who live near me just on a few streets. But the winters are cold, the wind shoots at you, cold on the legs. Not like here. You got to run for the streetcar – as fast as you can. Else your legs go numb. Nelly, the wife, loves it. She's from near there – Thunder Bay. She likes Toronto a lot. O, she wanted to come down here, but I thought it should wait, till I could fix things up for the summer, and then she could take it easy, like a queen, like, I mean she could have a decent place. She should wait. Someone's got to look after the house while Arnold and me is away."

The pastor decides it is the right time to get on the topic of morality and murmurs a few words about Ern.

"Um, Pastor, you're sure he died easy?"

"He was dead, stone dead, when I got there. Maud...she never called me, never got someone to go and fetch me. 'Twas young Obadiah's boy, come running..."

"Rodney?"

"No, it was young Kevin, he come running saying 'Ern's dead, he's dead, and his blood's all over the ground.' "

Obadiah gives a small laugh, and Amador nods. Now it's becoming a story and they settle in to listen. Amador goes to roll a smoke, but remembers the pastor and instead kicks at the floor and then picks at the frayed threads at the edge of his sleeves.

"Now what he really meant..." and the pastor is friendly now, he is into the story, and is watching Vince, and is listening to the broom sweep, and hears the voice of Billy Joe talking about the prices and hears the small bell ring over the store door, as someone else goes in and he doesn't have to look to know who it is, but pauses a second to identify the new voice, 'it's young Patsy', and he is back at the story, and the bell rings again as someone goes out. And then Billy Joe has finished his serving and he leans against the counter and listens through the brilloed hair of his ears to the preacher's voice, solid and able to carry over to the store counter.

"...was that there was red paint all over Ern. Because, as you know, Vince, he died painting the house, with a scarlet paint around the edges of the lovely white your father always used, and was sorry he couldn't see when he had gone blind. When I got there, Ern was red, and some of the paint was drying, o, even I thought he was like a sculped seal until I saw some drying quick and in peel, not like blood, and Maud was there with bread dough and flour all over her hands, and she clinging Ern to her bosom, getting mess all over the poor man's face. She stroking flour all over his face, and when I reached to get her away, she drove her fist at me. Yes, Vince, her fist, and then I had to get her away. I said, 'He's dead, Maud.' 'Not all your wishes are goin' to work,' says she. And I just stopped, for I was fond of Ern, and then I got her to shift, and looked after what had to be done, she just standing there, her hands hanging huge like two wet sacks of flour."

Amador is up on his feet, and moves towards the door, dying for a smoke. The preacher shifts to the side a little to let him by, and he goes past Billy Joe and hears the door behind him as he closes the latch. His ears still are held by the sound of the sweeping and the preacher's voice. Then the talk stops inside and his ears are rushed with the outside sound of the air all in a ring beating in his ears. In his hands is a package of Target tobacco. It's red, and a target like Robin Hood's is on the front.

The Vogue papers are as yellow as the cardboard cover with the line drawing of a woman's head on the side of the pack. Amador wonders if Nelly (put your belly) is like that Vogue cigarette lady, and if he kissed her slow and easy would she touch him as he touched her, and if when the lights were out.... He pauses and lights a cigarette, ashamed of his thinking going that way but then wonders if she'd like him better than Vince and he lights the smoke, and it's against his throat, and he coughs and spits, and then takes a good drag, and looks back in the store. The sun's coming up out of the clouds and the street is all over the window and he's got to shade with his hand and look and squint to see inside, and even then it's like the stove bunch are in the centre of a spot like when you breathe on a frosted pane, or in a calm part of a stream. Yes, 'like fishes,' he thinks and strains to hear the voices but gets mainly the sound of his heart in his ears, gives up and has his smoke at the wind.

"She was never meant..."

"Ern was. Did he still give a tune like he always did?"

"Could make the kindling dance," says Billy Joe from the counter where he's smoothin' the cat.

"My God, what a pair of ears," says Obadiah. Arnold is still whittling.

"O, Vince, I tried to get him to play that organ at service. The poor old thing with the stops gone, half them missing. Wouldn't have bothered Ern." The pastor looks sad. "He had the ear, and he had the gift. But he didn't use it. They were all musical."

"Lovely casket, as good as your Uncle Billy could have made, Vince. Clean in line and the shavings all over the floor, and the sweet smell of the wood shavings, and the way the plane moved true."

Arnold stops whittling, and looks up, confused. For one minute it's like he's back in Uncle William's shack again. The smell of the wood he's whittling helps keep him there for a second with the sound of the silence of his knife, like a stopped wood plane. The memory of how many times he was there helping. Never a word with Uncle William, just the scattered nod. Mostly they listened together to the sound of everything. The way the edge would move along the pine, the itch of the screws into the drilled holes, and the sound of the teeth on the gear of the drill as it turned, the sound of the wooden handle as it turned. Wasn't a lot to say, just listen. They never talked much there. Arnold is back in the store, and is looking at it back from the daydream.

When the phone rang telling Vince that Ern was dead, Nelly was watching Ed Sullivan on the neighbour's first TV. So there was no one home except Arnold with Vince. In the kitchen the electric kettle stopped the glub-glub, and Arnold was having the last of his ten cups of tea a day. It was just the perfect colour and just sweet and hot enough to dip a slice of toast into. Vince turned from the phone to say Ern is dead, an' it's as simple as the line of one of Uncle Billy's caskets. Ern is dead and they're on their way back home, the first time in years. Before they go, Arnold can hear Vince and Nelly talking, and Vince tells how he's going to get the house back.

Nelly doesn't care and can't see what the fuss is. In Vince's house Nelly had wallpapered the ceilings, and painted the walls brown, and had one painting of the ocean. The waves marbled up against some faded grey rocks, and a sunset shone in orange and red through the whole scene.

Her family hung in a series of photos along the stairway into the front hall. None of Vince's people showed up. Mainly because they didn't photograph well enough for Nelly, and neither herself nor Vince wanted any photos of near and dear relatives who were standing near casket shavings (or in the caskets themselves).

Nelly kept two small poodles, and she liked knitting small coats of red with black trim for them. Arnold once tried to kick one of them on the sly. It still managed to seize his leg with pointy teeth in the middle of a back flip. Nelly saw the whole thing, and for a while it looked like Arnold was going to be banished to the YMCA.

But Vince liked having him around. Without Arnold it was only him and Nelly. Nelly kept after Vince to take her to visit where he grew up. But he always came back with some excuse. Arnold always knew that Vince's real reason was Maud. Maud and Ern. Till one or both was dead there would be no going back for Vince. Among the pictures that never got on the family gallery section of the staircase there was one that Nelly had never seen. That was the picture of Maud. It was different than most pictures of the day. There was no painted sky in the background, no high-backed sofa, with Maud's arm leaned along the length of it. Instead there was Maud, as Maud-like as she could ever be, perched like a brooding hen on a picnic blanket 'longside of a burning fire. Over the fire, there were three longers gathered together, and a blackened tea kettle with the lid up, just on the boil.

Arnold used to wonder about that picture. Vince didn't like to talk about Maud, she was Ern's 'downfall', he'd say. Think of the house, the house of the Skipper, and Maud in the same bed with Ern that the old Skipper said his prayers by. But Arnold seized the thought like the poodle that had seized his leg. Why did Vince keep the picture? He finally decided that there was more to the whole thing than he knew and wondered if Vince could hate Maud more if he kept the picture handy. Sometimes he'd sneak a look into the family room and while Nelly was out to her club, Vince would be sitting by the fireplace, a big drink near him, and he looking at the picture.

Other times Arnold would watch Vince real close. It might be while there was a World Series game on the radio and they were in the backyard listening. When all of a sudden Vince's eyes would turn off and then, when they started up again, would be in a different mood, hate mixed in with memory.

Nelly always brought out drinks while the game was on and she'd put them on the small table by Vince's elbow, lean over and kiss him on the forehead but he'd shrug it off. "The game, listen, DiMaggio's up," and Arnold always wondered how Vince could keep track of that while he was daydreaming. Soon as Arnold got to daydream about the old days, that was it. He could be in the streetcar and away would go the car, the tracks, the sounds and smells and even a drunk sitting beside him and he'd be back in the cove or very tiny in the Skipper's house when the big voice yelled. There'd be no way he could tell where the trolley was and, more often than not, he'd come to and be five or six stops past where he was going and he'd have to try and get back to Simpson's if he could. That was where he worked as a night watchman. Along with a couple of other places.

Then he'd put on his uniform, changing in the basement. He'd lean against the locker. If no one else was there he'd put his face against the army cold of the metal and close his eyes and it would be like the feel of a winter morning at your face in the old house. Then while he moved around the store and punched the time clock, turned the key, he'd try to watch everything and forget his memories. Walk up the escalators and pretend that there were all kinds of people in the empty store. People like Amador and Obadiah would appear and he'd say, "O, here's where I keep my suits," and lead them through the men's department, and, "This is where I plays, when there's nothing else to do," and he'd start up the train sets, and watch their eyes go wide.

"Back at home…" and then he'd stop the thought and be aware of the place he really was.

"How was it at the store?" Nelly would ask when she'd see Arnold come in at breakfast.

"I'm real worried," he'd say and look real worried while she turned the bacon, and Vince hid behind the paper. "Real worried. No customers again last night." He and Nelly always got a good laugh over that one. And the first time Vince heard it he gave a laugh.

Nelly would smile and Arnold would wonder how a woman could ever look so thin. "Like Bessie," he'd think, and watch her tiny wrists, and little hands put the bacon on his plate. He'd watch the little veins in her earlobes and the way you could almost see through her neck. The way that when she walked she was going to break off and he'd wonder how she was married to Vince, and just think about how frail she looked. Vince called it genteel and was very proud of the way she looked. First, when he introduced her to Arnold, he was always taking him outside the restaurant to the cigarette machine or somewhere and saying, "She makes the ones at home look big and heavy and coarse. Breeding she got, breeding. You behave yourself, Arnold." And Arnold always did.

Nelly always seemed like she was going to shatter and when she talked, which was usually in bursts, he'd watch the ripples in her neck.

The stove door clangs shut, and Arnold's eyes are clearing and all around him Billy Joe's store is alive, and Amador rolls another smoke, and then palms it after a look from Pastor Roberts and the voices aren't back yet to full sound and Arnold smiles, because everyone is smiling at whatever the pastor said.

Chapter Nine

And now after the funeral day when the light is grey and early and the stuffed Canada goose in the sunporch window is looking wild in the wet grey light, Maud looks down at the fork in her hand. Maud feels it and for one second she is a child herself and small at the table. After that time she is back to the taste of the burn at the round of the bologna, the feel of greasy toast crumbs rolling the round of her lips, and the listen of all the kitchen sounds that creak and hiss, and crack around her. The sounds that join the inside to the outside, the roll of the grey air and the horn now starting against the fog; the oo-gaah horn against the bank of the fog. The sound of a horse and the voices of children being pried from bed.

She looks out and sees Sue on the road and moves back to pull the kettle from the warming part of the stove to where it can boil again and she can weaken the too strong steep of black tea.

She looks to the wall where the fiddle of Ern still hangs and she misses, like it was years ago instead of days, the near and the now of him, the creak of the stairs. And most of all the way he could let the fiddle do the talking for him, let any music be his tongue. The light of fiddle or the keen of saw, as he bent and cut the air with notes sad as spun glass in the hands. "O Lord, how far away he be and how near."

Sue is at the door.

"Sue, my love, come in, me dear."

And the latch lifts, the string slipping back through the top of the latch holes.

"My God," thinks Maud, "how the age of Sue is on her this morning, her hair in strands, as always, poking every which way. 'Birch broom in the fits,' Ern used to say."

"Morning, Maud. Dampish."

Sue, the knot on her bandanna tied so tight she can't pick it apart with her fingers, has on gum boots that are cut ankle high, and over the top of them you can see bright blue socks rolled down, and over the top of the socks, nylons short and rolled.

She has a little belly like a pigeon and her ass sticks out. She is seventy-five and hasn't had a birthday for years. Her glasses are steamed with the kitchen and she gropes for a chair with one hand and runs fingers a-smear over the lens with the other.

Her forehead has tiny wrinkles and under her eyes the flesh is loose and drops. Her eyes are grey, fog over ice. Ice edge melting.

She tips hot tea off the saucer to her lips and is sitting and talking all at once, while her free hand ties the knot on her bandanna.

"O, Maud, the damp is the rheumatiz of me. I saw Pastor Roberts, he in the car. After the funeral, Vince next to him, arms pointing at this and that, and sometimes they'd get excited and they both gets out of the car, with arms pointing, fingers waving. God, his cheeks are red and rough like house-maid's knees. Maud, how is you feeling, maid? If there is any words...."

Maud is trying to figure out how she can work a few words around to say something, but her tongue is slippery, and the words fall off as she tries to tell her about how she woke up sitting in bed and thought she could hear the fiddle and wanted Ern back, knew where he was but wondered if it was him, and froze to the thoughts of a ghost of him, and prayed for it. And toes a-curl was over the steps 'til scared she thought the music was in the upstairs, 'til with a start she was wide awake in bed sitting upright and no music, and it was a dream.

Maud sets the kettle back to the warm of the stove where the back burners are still the shine of Imp stove polish. The devil on the package looks out with a sparkle to his pitchfork.

"And what was Vince looking at? Was Arnold there?"

"Yesterday, Vince was lookin' down at the flakes, later he were by Billy Joe Simmonds' store, then by the cliffs, and last they was lookin' here, before the light went down last night, and they, he and Arnold, was over to the Pastor's house. He took them in and his sports coat, against his shoulders, tight like knots on rope, and Vince with his shoulders heavy under the arm, leading Arnold, who's on the lope like an old dog."

Chapter Ten

Sue is looking out the window at the old women, all widow -black on the flakes, they with their white aprons, and all fitting and turning like crows and seagulls.

"No one 'cept Ern ever blamed Vince for leaving, Maud." Sue paused.

"Ern was the one had to spoon that soft egg into the old man's mouth. The skipper was blind then. The old man would talk on and on about Vince, and sometimes about Arnold. Talk and talk with the egg running down through the stubble, and Ern watchin' with his stomach half turned."

Sue is back from the window and as she turns to Maud, the women on the flakes are over her shoulder, and for Maud the angle makes it look like the bitty people are all perched on Sue's shoulder. She wants to tell her but Sue is onto the talk and has started again.

"He'd say the same things to Bessie, too."

"I don't care what he was like with Bessie! Wasn't only me what lost patience. Ern lost patience too."

"As well he might."

"He wished the old man dead."

"Now Maud, that's not true."

"No?"

"I s'pose Bessie didn't feel the same way? O, I wonders why Vince is back."

"You knows the answer to that." And Maud looks around.

"That's easy. His brother is dead, Arnold and Vince is here for the funeral."

"Arnold might be along for the funeral....But Vince himself, o, he's here for more. For somethin' else."

"Like what?"

"You're standing on it. On the floor of it."

"The kitchen? The house?"

And Sue laughs. She takes in the laugh and her back buckles to the sway of it, her feet tip on the floor, and she slaps her knees on the sides.

"Maud, my maid, what would he want with a place like this? Less he floats it up to Toronto on barrels."

"Why else would he be here? He got something to prove to me."

Sue thinks about this – she sits on the daybed. "I s'pose we won't be havin' the talks like we used to before."

"Why not?"

" 'Cause I guess you'll have to go. Vince got rights. You got none, you'll have to go home. 'Tisn't like you're married...no need to look at me that way. I know 'twas the same thing, but maid, you'll have to go home."

"Sue, don't you know me better than that?"

"I knows you, but Maud, there'll be a racket. An' a bigger racket than you ever seen."

"I don't mind rackets."

"Ah, then you had Ern to fight along with you. Now he ain't here, an' you got most of this place against you. They still hate seeing someone come in and replace another man's wife. Especially without marrying. You been spitting in their faces every day with what you been doing."

"Trouble is I didn't spit hard enough."

Maud's shoulders are so tight with anger that she can feel the muscles roll over her backbone, over her shoulder blades. She lets them feel tight and she tightens them even more, and then relaxes them like the memory of picking up and setting down full buckets of water.

"Maud, you got a saucy tongue. The pastor is dead against you and Vince got the rights of being the first born. You know the Skipper's stuff is his."

Maud looks around the kitchen. 'Tis hers. On one wall there is a shelf of pine wood with varnish that shines like glass. There is a clothes line strung the length of the kitchen and towels and worsted socks absent-minded like are hung the half way of it. All of Ern's fishing socks are hanging there.

The floor is peeling linoleum and where one hole has worn through there's another left-over-bit slid underneath, showing like tired piss-a-beds, the dandelion flowers all a-shine. The door to the porch has cloth nailed to it, and drafts make it sway. The window has a pull blind with white lace near the edge. An old pipe is dotted near some old 'baccy, the rough edge of broken off plugs of *Club* chewing tobacco.

"This is my kitchen," says Maud.

And Sue, "Of course it is, maid. A good and warm kitchen.

Maud walks to the stove. She's a woman who knows the weight of her steps and they are firm with a sideways canter to them that comes from the sea. Her feet float around when she's in a chair. When she sits, her knees are splayed and her ankles are together. Maud is in her mind a widow. In the mind of George's Cove she is not.

She moves to the wall and takes down the fiddle, hand shined and touched with the dance of rosin off the bow. The bow itself, no frayed strings, but worn and shiny with wear and rosin to just the right bounce. She tunes and tries to play the fiddle, bringing back the jig and reel of him, the sound now of "Sweet Forget Me Not." The song that on that fog of a day does slip under the door and make whoever hears the tune think of Ern. Sue and Maud think on Ern as the music spills around the kitchen and Maud remembers Bessie, her hands as delicate as a tea cup. Bessie's fingers long as sea weed, and white as bones on the beach.

Maud thinks that when Bessie moved, o, then her own steps were heavy and tired upon the floor, great side of beef a-rest against the wall, great blood-stain of a blush that lights the wall.

In her mind, Maud is now a widow. The house that Ern looked after because Vince couldn't make it back home was now her house.

George's Cove must be an old place. Older than anyone's memory because all she can think about are the look of the rocks, the fences all fallen down with a twist along them, the root cellars grown in and the grass in the lines of where the first church was.

The church was made with iron nails and wood pegs. It was small and white, and when you walked in for Sunday morning service, there was in early years a small lawn you walked by and in later years some new and very clean tombstones. Later they were old and cracked and gone yellow and to the salt air so long that if you had licked them, your tongue would saltlick back in the start of it. The inside of the church had benches of dark varnished wood with the seats a hymn-book-and-a-half wide and the back of the pew titled ahead so if you dozed it was crash on the floor. There was an organ that required the air of many pumpings and made notes that hung around the lamps that from the ceiling dangled. Sometimes the lamps smoked, and the ceiling had gone grey with the washings of soot-filled days. The windows were of plain glass and the small stove in the church's middle ate wood fast enough to keep small boys running, and cold were the hands of those to start it and hot the backs of those who sat just before it.

John Green, the first of the men from Devon, did preach a Methodist-preaching from the plain pulpit. His hands were big enough to hold the words he spoke. Always his arms flung over long at the front row, and wrists came about a foot out of his sleeves. He was one of eight men who made the town and all his preachings stayed for a long time, and the church of his dreams died in dry and in wet rot, and under the salt of the air, and the blow of the wind so strong that even a steel cable couldn't hold the roof on.

That was until Pastor Roberts arrived in the cove. Came first with what looked like a circus tent. The pastor, his wife and daughter all struggled with the tent in the wind that never stopped blowing. And all the children on their way home from school stopped by to watch the flapping and the billowing of the tent. They stood near-far on the teeter of shyness as the pastor called out hearty and loud no matter how the tent shifted. His daughter carefully looked away from all the children and she was torn. as always, between shyness and pride at being the centre of all the looks. The wife faded in and out of sight blending with the beige of the tent. She always was like that it turned out later, fading in and out, next to the bluff and the hearty, the shouters and the yellers and the thick eyebrows of her husband, she was not noticed a lot.

By the time the grownups got near and started shifting from one foot to the other, or sitting on large rocks a distance from the tent, smoking and watching, or having hands in apron pockets, the tent was up and ropes were hooked over notched pegs in the ground, the flap of the entrance curled in and out like a tongue, until it finally sidled outside and stayed pressed against the tent; an apron blown across a dress. Then the girl and the woman unfurled the sign, done in yellow and orange on a black background... "The Gospel Tent ... In His Name." It was the first ever from outside preacher of that sort the people in the cove had ever seen. So that night the tent was packed by the curious and by those, as Pastor Roberts said, who were thirsty for the drink that quenches. Eight o'clock was the time for the service and that was the time that the latest got there. There was a smell of toilet water, of bay rum and the look of scrubbed faces, and rough hands given an extra good scouring. The lanterns hung from the centre pole jiggled, and those on supports near the door swayed.

The tent bulged in and out, its canvas touching the back of those who arrived late and the smell of wax and of lamp-heat was everywhere. In the centre was a pulpit and soon the pastor was stalking around it preaching the fires of Hell and the cool waters of Heaven to everyone.

At first his way was so different that people wanted to laugh and Amador even let out a chuckle, which he at once regretted as the pastor stamped towards him, and described in detail the hot kind of Hell that was reserved for those who laughed at the Lord's ways. Ern walked out, and Maud was next behind. Bessie stayed and so did everyone else and soon there was nothing funny in the words, and soon people had tears down their cheeks and they were telling everyone their sins and all the children marvelled at the wicked things their parents were doing. Then it was prayer. Then everyone was stumbling along the paths to home, and even the children were quiet. Everyone was glad of the dark, so in homes everywhere that night they wondered and figured they might get over it. Some thought that in relief, others were scared that it might come true for they were warmed by the Lord. Bessie and Ern had a row and Ern went and got drunk. Bessie cried herself to sleep and, from her attic room, Maud heard Ern come home singing a filthy song about a cat. She smiled and went to sleep thinking that Pastor Roberts would soon be gone. But he never left.

They stayed on and on. The sons all looked like the father. The same shoulders and neck and they all clutched bibles to their chests, and sang harmony in the Mission. One played the accordion, another played guitar, and the other sang along almost on key. The church was named the Gospel Church and the people had their favourite stories of temptation and salvation which they got to polish up over the years. They were always glad to give them with pride when called on.

The cove began to be a gospel cove and the people bought new antenna wire for their radios so they could hear the Hour of Decision on a Sunday evening, as they ate bread and jam, and jellied salads, and cold green peas from Libby's cans. And they prayed and they disapproved of things they never paid much mind to before. Sunday was real quiet, so quiet that you could hear early morning gospel and breakfast sounds from each house if you were out on the road, and walked by. Sometimes Maud did that; the sound of the radio would fade down as you walked past one house, and the same hymn or sermon would rise up again as you came close to another house.

The cooking was quick, because everything was prepared the night before. In white enamel pans the cut-up potato, carrots, cabbage, and turnip were hidden, and white cloth over the water stillness of the cut vegetables. The salt-beef would be in soak all ready to put in the pot, or the cut of beef ready, or the hen, killed and cleaned, and plucked the night before, all the linoleum drifted by the feathers and jewelled by the tiny drops of blood, and before midnight the homes would smell of singeing where the burning stick was laid along the plucked hens to smoke away the pin feathers. And children, if they were good, had the hen claws with the tendon left long so they could pull on it and make the claws close and open. Small boys would chase small girls until they would run from the boys pretending to be scared, until all kicked up so much racket that they were sent to bed and the claws thrown on the dying coals banked for the night. Then the claws would close up as they quivered in the heat.

George's Cove had gone different. And though the dances still kept on, and Ern still shouted out about playing "Snot on the Chicken's Lip", there was a difference. At least on the surface and that was where it mattered most. That was where the nods didn't go friendly; that was where the backs would turn; that was where the hellos stopped. And even if it was still the same underneath, it didn't really matter.

Now Maud's house can be seen from the wharf. It stands by itself in the middle of a small field. There is one wind-combed tree next to the house. Next to that there is a grey woodshed, with a white circle painted on it. On the roof is a weathervane with a rooster on top. The path goes by the well, and roams down to the stages where the fish are landed. The white picket fence glows.

In winter the sea doesn't freeze, all that happens is the colour goes grey and the snow can skid across the waters, and doors are closed against the wind and lamp-lit windows are vortexed by a swirl of snow and all the snow flakes go dizzy.

The face of Maud is looking out the window into spring, and Sue moves through the fog to the well. She doesn't run but walks like a fly on butter. In the mud she holds herself very still against the slip-and-fall. She carries a galvanized pail which has an odd-looking rope tied to it, the splice around the bucket's handle. The splash of bucket tips over to its side and the water flows in.

Inside Billy Joe Simmonds' store, there's a smell of apples and of Dustbane and scent of peppermint knobs and lassie kisses, with the rich of *Club* and *Beaver* tobacco and the smell of dry goods. There are grey and red worsted socks, and the brown of breeches.

The counter is made of dark wood, and notched by the young ones testing out their pearl-handled pocket knives. The brown roll of paper held by filigreed reed arms is tearing for another customer, and Billy Joe twists round his hand's centre the string and the ball by the ceiling spins and snaps and bursts the twine. It is as sure as the tug that takes just enough for the parcel, and it shakes the string ball, and the parcel is as neat and packaged as a liver folded inside a sheep.

O, Billy Joe runs this store and no matter what the stove people think as they talk important and as persistent as a bluebottle; for Billy, the people by the stove are not the centre of the world nor even near the edge of it. This store that once was his father's.

Now the buzz stops for a second and in the store it's as quiet as a snowflake on a mitt.

"Pastor, tonight we'll be staying somewhere else."

Arnold stirs and stares.

"Vince, my son, what's wrong with my place? There's nowhere else you should stay. I won't have it."

"My house."

There is a pause, and thoughts around the stove, and Billy Joe nods his head. The pastor thinks a bit longer than the others, and though most everyone else has come to their own conclusions, they still manage to look like they're considering what was just said while they wait for the pastor to talk.

"You were the first born, Vince."

"Yes, by a year or two."

"Your father leave a will?"

"No, Ern just took the house."

Arnold sits up straight.

"Father said Ern was to have it."

"That's only what Ern said, but Ern is gone, and I'm first-born."

The pastor stands up and stretches. And moves towards the door. Vince starts to get up, and Arnold is quick as he moves over by the counter and buys a handful of peppermint knobs to keep him over until he knows what's going to happen.

The pastor is out and moving towards the first and the only car in the cove. It is an Austin with real leather seats and the smell when the door is opened is as good as slipping on gloves against the cold. In the winter like gloves left outdoors or in the cold of the outside porch.

The car is black, and the dash is of wood and rubbed to a burled shine. The shift has double-low and in that car you could pull up stumps. The car is high and the running boards can hold the weight of a fair-sized man. People could be and sometimes are carried there. The motor grinds and the pastor,

Vince, and Arnold are bouncing over the widened path, the car lists sideways and climbs small hills like a turtle. Sometimes the leather is so slippery and the climb so steep that Arnold slips and can't see out the window. From the outside the car is so slow that you could walk alongside it and stare at Vince, which some people do for a while. The window is rolled down, and his arm is elbowed outside. He's smiling and watches mainly to his right.

The pastor drives the car like he's tacking a boat. His arms are straight out in front of him and he is pried up over the seat so as to see the road better. He looks to neither side but stares straight ahead. He doesn't like changing gears and spends most of this time in double low, or maybe up to low or second in a reckless moment. He moves across, instead of around, curves and sometimes will stop altogether while he figures out which way to go.

They bounce and roll towards the pastor's house. Sheep are nudged aside while chickens run.

Vince is bouncing and all the town is rocking back and forth as he thinks of his house and the years of it that are still locked inside the walls. He is thinking of the look on Maud's face and how he will tell her what he has to tell her. Her face is not the face he saw at the funeral. Her face is the face of twenty years ago.

Ern always stood off to the side, unless the old man wanted music. Then he would move in close to the Skipper's chair. He would tune the fiddle so quick that even the different sounds of the tuning moved into one blur of a chord that started off the song that suited the mood of the Skipper.

The old man never let his face change nor in any way let Ern know that the tune was to the mood.

Vince knew and he watched Maud. Sometimes she'd be dusting and the feather duster would take on the beat of the music, would swirl around and Vince saw the way she'd press her hip against the dresser, or against the hall stand, and the way Vince knew, he just knew she was waiting for it by the way her eyes would half shut.

Ern always played with his eyes closing, then finally full-shut as he leaned into the music, hunkered down on the notes. He always claimed if you could play a song all the way through without shutting your eyes, why then you weren't part of the song and if you weren't part of the music, "then" said Ern again, "what was the point of playing it – might as well go milk the goats."

All the time Vince thought he knew by the way Maud leaned against the music too, the way she stroked her hand lightly along her face as the music was soft and the fiddle high and a-tremble, by the way that she could never keep away from the sound of the string, or the quiver of the saw like a tongue on salt that she was waiting and Vince could wait too. He had plenty of time.

Vince would try to talk with Maud. "O Maud, that's a fine way you have of moving."

"Yes, b'y, on two feet, first one then the other, sometimes I goes left to right, 'stead of right to left."

"You know what I mean. You're a woman."

"You got anything better to do with your time? Like counting connors?"

"You might spend some more time looking after the house and tending to Father. He needs more help and the way you handle him, he's always saying you're too rough. He complains. He complains to you."

Maud looked at Vince in that time of twenty years ago, and now is in Vince's mind between bumps, and she was very still. Her anger made her heavier, thickened her ankles, her face, her neck. To the eye of Vince she became common. Her face crude, her lips too thick, her nose rough and her looks scrubbed raw. Her soap was on her, and her cheeks were like a plank before the sanding goes to it. Her eyes were too black with hate, and her throat was strong with words that would sound wrong, would sound so heavy that they would fall to the floor.

"Maud, sometime Father's gonna be dead, and I'll be in charge of this place, and I don't want someone heavy and a crash round the corner near me or near the place. You got a lot to learn. A lot to learn... that they never learned you at home."

"Vince, if you was a man, I'd have put a frying pan through your head. I'd gut you like a cod."

Maud turned and walked away, her anger left behind in the room even though she'd gone. Her anger like bile and Sunlight soap all mixed up. Vince looked at his own reflection in the glass before the dishes, and walked closer to look in the lusterware, his eyes curved back, but Vince knew he looked good. He made himself look even angrier, drew the anger still loose in the room to his face, and felt the hate make his face look strong and hard, his eyes as cool as ice in the stream, and he imagined Maud scared, and moving away, on backward steps as scared as pinfish when a big hand comes in the water.

Pastor Roberts' voice comes through, and they are now at the pastor's house and Arnold is already out of the car. The pastor's face is puzzled.

"Arnold, I knows 'tis hard the way Ern was taken away." But Arnold doesn't look back. The pastor shakes his head and looks even more puzzled.

Now Arnold is walking up the hill. The tire marks have worn at the grass. It is ankle high. Arnold walks on the left track for a while and then starts walking back from one track to the other making z's in the path. He pretends it's a railway track, and then he's turning left towards Maud's and there he is walking in almost knee-high hay in some old field. "Mrs. King's," he thinks, and the last of the longers that made up the fence have fallen down and they are grey, even the rot is grey and no longer the surprise of brown or gold rot.

His grip hurts his hand so he shifts it over. Now he pauses and looks back at the pastor's house. It is big and painted a buff yellow with green trim. The Union Jack is all stiff and buckles in the wind that yells off the cliffs, and brings with it hidden ice, that can take some jigging line and ice it so the side of the dory is thick, and sawed with heat of it when the jigging gets faster, and covered with the rime of it when the jigging slows and stops. Arnold wonders about Vince but then his mind gets caught up with the "here I am now" of the place, and "here was I once", and the two are different, and he thinks the thought of every homeowner of how the place has shrunk and thinks that he is the first to think it.

His mind is caught up with the chop-chop-chop of an axe and the almost metal sound that makes him think Maud is cleaving birch, and then in his mind is the memory of her young with a stick across her shoulders and a bucket at either end of the stick.

"Yes, 'tis her cleaving the birch," he thinks, and she looks up and sees him. And Maud sees Arnold like a warp of memory of Arnold-the-child. He still has the hands – too awkward to lie near the ends of his arms. They are like great moths fluttering to the light-holding lint all over his suit. Arnold tries to think of what he's going to say to Maud – something that doesn't cling to memory. Something as proper and solid as the clink of the axe cleaving the wood.

Now he stands in the yard. The old chopping block has gone grey with the weather; through spring putting the heave to it with a crowbar of ice and water; through summer slipping it into the oven. O, there was the sweet grain of heat, and cold wound all around it like ice on a line salt rimed over through the night, and grass taking the blades to the side.

"Maud, you looks as strong, as good as you ever done."

Chop, clink, shake, the axe high again. Then the sound stops and the echoes die down.

"Vince is going to come here, Maud. He's gonna stay – and me too, though I'm asking."

Maud stops and Arnold sits by the chopping block. Sits on a half decent size log.

Maud lifts up the biggest of the chunks of wood and carrying them tight to her breast, starts belly forward. So much wood in her arms that the ache is moving along her legs shifts to her back, and along the shoulders and neck. Not a word does she say of Vince nor of the way the thought of Vince is fog in the day. The strain of carrying the wood is tipping her into a moment of sideways walking while her breasts rest on a sheet of muscle, her toes pause like something planted and she heaves the wood to the growing pile near the wood shed.

She picks up the axe again – its handle the same warm colour as the chopping block and warm as the wax that drops from the candle to the hand when it's being carried towards a dark hall. Now, down comes the axe and it hits wood and a knot in the wood crashes through the arms the vibrations; it's like hitting a rod of iron to the hearts of an anvil. But before the blade can be grabbed by the closing wood, she rocks the blade up and out.

Arnold watches. Remembering when he was ten years old, the look of Maud working her arms as she hoisted the well bucket, as she chopped wood, and as she baked bread. The memory of her baking bread is so strong that he smells the hot yeast smell of a growing crust hung in the air near his head, and feels hungry and watches Maud, while the smell is pinned with the sharp clip clop of the axe to the wood.

He thinks on the bread and remembers how, a small boy, he would watch the look of her as she kneaded the bread, her breasts shifting too and seeming to spread as she reached back and then pushed down on the dough 'til she would pause and dip her hand in the small bowl of flour and dust, dust the table, the raw wooden table, and Arnold would cross to the other side and squint and pretend it was a snowstorm.

He was only a lean small boy then as strong as an eel all muscle and with a heart as large as a baby's. When he was in that kitchen and the bread baking (o, the memory was growing warm as butter), he could dance on the heat from the stove, the hot bread to the butter on waxed paper that smoothed over its top. Then back in that kitchen, Maud, so happy with this small boy who watched her every move, kissed him a blessing and pinched his cheek. He, later in the looking-glass, stared at the flour on his cheeks. The only mark of the kiss, the sign of the blessing, except for that place in the mind where he saved it for lonely times and brought it out in the cold of a Toronto winter to warm.

Sometimes the place where he thought of the memory would be warm, and then he thought of it in a different way. He could be in a bar where there was smoke and warm beer smell enough to set a beer glass on only to have it drift in a slow rolling tumble down the rolls of the smoke shape. There he still felt lonely, at the edge of all the talk and laugh and light. He would think of the kitchen back home and would look like his eyes were going glassy, while inside his mind he would watch the flour drift across a table that was made of plain wood.

In the yard, the wood leaps apart, and Maud has sweat on the back of her dress, the shape of a moth on the back, and asks only "Is he?"

She adds, sensing that Arnold is waiting to hear more, "I s'pose you wants to stay. Well, Arnold, my son, you're welcome. I can even see some of Ern in your face, sometimes the way you was watching me I even saw little bits of the way his eyes useta look. Come in, my son, and bring some wood. Maybe we could burn the suitcase, there's more of that than wood!"

As they enter the home, Arnold sees, to his surprise, that the house has shrunk a good deal. All the ceilings are lower, the nailed wood criss-crosses inches below where his head tops. All the doorways are exactly Maud's height, and Ern's too, he thinks. Then he remembers that Ern wasn't that short, and pauses a second.

"Maud, Ern must have been awful squat up in here."

"Yes, Arnold, only chance he got to stretch out was in the casket."

Arnold laughs, the laughs grabbed out of him. Maud bursts goblets of laugh – so warm and loud the room is full and Arnold is held in by the laugh, all is inside the laughing, as warm and round as a dust ball under a feather bed.

She takes the suitcase from him and swings it in an arc up the stairs, till it pitches upright and shivers in the cool of the upper hall.

"You knows where your room is, Arnold."

And now in that room, where the ceiling tilts from right to left all forty-five degrees by the roof and the floor tips the other way, for a second it's like getting on a boat when there's a lop on. The bed is still there, the same, except most likely more lumpy and much damper.

The brown hollow rolled tin is a half moon shape at the head of it, and over that a large Sunday school picture of Jesus. He in a gown that was white when the picture was hung, but now has gone sepia and yellow, and the Lord's hair all gone brown, and kind of green where the mildew is doing its work, and the light from heaven that had shone down in a golden glow, had the colour drained out of it by any sunbeam that chanced to touch the picture over the years. Now it was as white and pure as snow. The eyes were still the same. When Arnold was small he could have sworn that the eyes stared at him, and most likely stayed open all night, a thought that gave him trouble in his adolescence.

The bed's tin legs had given way some time ago, and the whole frame had been replaced by a wooden one. It was done by Uncle William and so was done well. Arnold could imagine the shavings sweet and clean, like candy. The wood had over the years been given so many coats of varnish that it turned black, and then to jet black, it held pools of light even deeper than the polished top of the woodstove. Arnold is thinking his way to the feelings of a small boy knee-deep in his gum boots in a flooded pond of shavings. Golden curls of wood where Uncle William was talking and using the plane. Slip swirl the sound of the plane until it clogged and was cleared by his uncle slipping the curls onto Arnold's head, where they hooked and tore as Arnold tried to haul them out to look at them.

The Skipper moved over and loaned Arnold his pocket knife.

"You keep that now for a while."

Uncle William grinned, "G'way boy, no way you'll get that back, that's Arnold's. Now you hold that in your little mitt, my lovely, and remember it's yours no matter what the Skipper says."

The Skipper gave Uncle William a dirty look, but Arnold knew the knife was his to keep.

Uncle William tossed him a piece of pine to whittle on, and Arnold took the knife, the weight of it on his hand. He opened the blade, prying with his finger nail till the blade that his father could open one-handed, slowly opened. The little steel holders still snuggled the handle to the metal, and were as shiny as the blade itself which was honed to a dangerous edge all whetstone and white.

Arnold tried to make the wood curl, his first cuts straight down, and arm away, because he had watched so many times all his uncles. But he couldn't make shavings so he cried and the two men laughed and then right by his head was the moustache of Uncle William, with the smell of *Club* tobacco all through it. He took Arnold's hands and put one on the wood, the other to the knife.

"O, Arnold, lad, you got such a strong hand for one so small. But to be a carpenter, the touch must be light. Let the wood do the work, go with the grain and the knife finds the path. See, see, the wood it likes to curl up, likes to bend, there, there, just go with the wood, let the knife feel the way. There...save the strength."

And before that day had ended, Arnold made curl after curl almost as fine as the plane itself.

Back in the room, Arnold now wonders what ever happened to that knife. Is it hiding in Toronto in the crawl space? That spot where his tools are hiding; vaseline-covered to keep away the grey join of red rust, and old bleed of spatter on metal.

"What is it?" asks Maud, and her voice is so like the memory of a wood curl, that he almost tells her. But his voice isn't used to speaking real things too often. It has grown rusty, not used much. "O, Maud," he thinks, "if for one or two minutes I could talk then I might never stop. The words would fill the room like shavings, and still talking I could feed them to the stove, and we could talk on and on, still warm, still talking, till the stove was white hot and the night blacker as the wood smell took to the clouds."

"Arnold, you look sad." Why Arnold, are you wishing that Vince had been sent far away to sea, had been hit by your father's hand of snakes (eels under the skin)? Old yellow skin as yellow as cat's piss on snow.

In the kitchen it is an hour later, and Maud has a large heavy knife. "So Vince is coming here," she thinks, and tests the knife before she starts supper. The blade is tipped against her thumb, cat's claw in and out. Vince. She sharpens the knife, the blade is dull. Now water on the whetstone, scrape, scratch, swish, and scratch; the whetstone is catching in the deep of the metal the touch that can peel skin like lifting skin from an onion. The edge is slippery and hard to find, and when it's there the second after it wasn't and the second before it goes you have to stop.

"And what does it mean?" wonders Maud, between the slap and the slip of grit of whetstone back into the sheath,

"Vince coming here? And before the knife is cutting Maud touches her tongue to the edge of the whetstone and now it feels like the grit is still doing a granite rolling along her tongue. The stone goes back in its black leather case and the knife is on the salt beef, cutting, clean and sharpfast. Arnold makes sense, but Vince, and what's he doing with the pastor? Did some burst of light hit Vince – get his mind and heart and send him back home to be saved by the pastor? She thinks of the day he left George's Cove.

Vince in his suit and Arnold lugging that great suitcase, same one he lugged out of here when he went. Funny he still was two steps and one to the side behind Vince. The *Northern Ranger* was late the day they left. Vince's hands on the suitcase where Arnold had set it down were dry and neat, like undertaker's hands. The suit was new. Too small and never before worn. The blue had a light stripe, wide lapels like on the suit they would use to dress the Skipper. Tight-lipped Vince was smoking Target tobacco, rolled in a Vogue paper. The smoke was rolled lean and tight so as he had to keep puffing or it would have gone out. Vince thought it would fool people into believing the smoke was a tailor made. That's all he knew about the mainland in them days. Arnold looked too young to smoke. But this time he had rolled himself a fat cigarette. His tobacco bulged towards the centre where the glue didn't hold. He was smoking, and looking around like the Skipper was there to see him. Maud was standing by Ern near the edge of the wharf. She leaned on the piling. It was red and white with paint peeled by the salt. Vince looked towards the sea and saw the fog was light. He blew the smoke towards the fog; the fine taste of rolled tight tobacco. Arnold ran his hand back along his hair to feel the pompadour still greased in place.

Then a blast of horn and the boat was in and small boys scattered as the rope was tossed to the wharf. The men grasping and flinging the noose around the pilings, and the boys who had come near again, now ran back as fast as they could. There wasn't a one of them but had heard the story of the boy who stayed near one of these tensing ropes. The pressure had snapped the hawser, and it coiled around the boy's neck like a whip, and flipped his head overboard, leaving only the stump of a spouting body behind. Each boy remembered that story.

Vince stood there without moving, trying to blow smoke rings into the light wind. Arnold looked at the ropes and stepped back a pace. And that was the day they had left the cove – it took Ern's death to bring the two of them back.

Chapter Eleven

Vince has time alone in the spare bedroom at the pastor's house "to freshen up," Mrs. Roberts said. The buzz of the pastor's family, like flies on fish, crawls under the door of his room. The pastor's daughter Ruth has a voice sweet enough to be different. It seems more to be present in the pauses, which God knows are few enough. Then Ruth's voice sounds like the lazy drawl of a bee. Vince is looking in his suitcase. Between clothes – and wrapped in a towel, there is a photo. The frame is wooden, hand made, and the glass is crazed with a thin web of cracks, moving from the lower lefthand corner.

The photo itself is faded, and is of Maud. A much younger Maud. She's by the currant bushes – the ones that run wild into black and red, near the gooseberry patches, pale-eye green. Striped. Maud has just taken a handful of berries, and they're spilling from the edge of her hand to her mouth. The snap was sketched just as the berries started to fall, and there is in her eyes delight at the berries, at the so many of them that they will fall and not be picked up. For years Vince has kept this photo along with the picnic photo. The look on his face over the years has changed each time he looked at the picture. Now he knows just how Maud will end up, how that smile and delight will really come to mean nothing after the years have dropped. The house will go and Maud will leave, and even then she will have nowhere to go. Ern's dead and that's too bad. Yes, Ern is dead.

So the house will be Vince's – just like the Skipper really wanted. The boards will go on the windows, the doors will be nailed fast and the inside will be left as it is – as it was. Caught like a snapshot, sketched into the stillness that will hold it, caught in webs, and with carpenter bugs crawling, black shells on the floor, until they, too, dry up, their little legs like dust specks, and the final curl of their death, rolled into little black circles. Dust balls will be quiet and grey and they will quiver to the shifts of the mice. Rats will chew their way through the walls and look for food. They will stay till there is nothing left to eat, no paper, no leather, no left crumbs, and they will go, and only the light and the dark will stay. The sun shuttered by the heaving boards on the window will shine through the summer, and the scattered winter's day of sun blue yellow – the floor will curl and brittle push, then will crack because of the ice and heat, the furniture will cuddle hoar frost, and will mildew, and be rat nested to thinness. The winter will grow ice, the summer will grow bugs.

Vince thinks of himself back in Toronto, where sometimes in the busy of Yonge Street the horns and the traffic would warp and shimmer while the sound would drain from the street, all the cars would move in slow motion, and the edges of his vision would come in and he would stop his walking, until bumped from behind, and then he would walk over to a store window to pretend he was looking in the window, but really using the window for an escape, a way back to the younger face of Maud.

And the hate-love of the face is there before him. If only it had been Ern who had thrown her out – even then she with no place else to go. If Ern had cheated on her and made her sad, so sad that she had just sneaked away one night.

If Ern had said, "Vince, boy, you're my brother, we got to stick together." Then Vince wouldn't have to be here at the funeral. With Ern under the ground, slush on his grave.

Now Maud would suffer, would leave, and then the house that should have been his will be. It always should have been his. He was the oldest. Maybe he would burn it down, or just stay for a while on the inside of the house, never to be seen again and everyone would forget he was in there. And he could sneak around and check the windows, and of an evening sit in the Skipper's chair and pretend, in the dark, to be the Skipper.

In the pastor's house, Vince hasn't talked much but he sure has listened. Not so much to the content of the pastor's comments but to something else, the Methodist gone wrong that's hiding in the words. The dark and the strong hateful way that can become rightful indignation at sinners. Especially unrepenting sinners. The house creaks back that feeling. It is so strong that every dark coloured book on the shelves, each picture on the wall – even the brightly coloured picture of the gospel ship – radiates hate and the tenseness of a house that waits for any wrong move; the statement that is suspect; the hint of rebuke from the wife; the move of a daughter that might be sensual. Anger, peeking from behind the grate, from boys who would leap as soon as they could to be free.

The pastor has long cold fingers, cold and clamped, like gravediggers' in the winter. His hair is thinning, and the skull that shows is as white as salted ice. No matter how often he shaves his face is blue. His eyebrows are thick as coal dust, and his neck is webbed. There is a feeling that his eyes are always open, and at night could shine like a lighthouse through a room.

This man, this pastor, can hate. Maud was the main mote and still is in his eye.

"How soon, how soon?" he asks the Lord. "How soon can she be hove out?"

Maud was like molldow on dying trees, the fine green tendrils dried out to tangled thread with small snowflakes of old bark caught in the tangles. It's as hard to pluck the thoughts of Maud away as to take out all the specks of bark in a forest of molldow. Every time he thinks of Maud his fingers pluck and are restless as a dying man's nails on an afghan. But the pastor can't make her leave his eyes, his thoughts.

Each Sabbath the church holds his thoughts. All the raw faces and red ears listening to his talk of sin. The congregation of huge hands on the black of the hymnbooks or the rough red small hands twirling wedding bands, stroking the heads of idle children, or flicking imaginary lint off blue serge suits. The community has become God fearing, but the worm thought is at him... But what of Maud? Her sin, her eyes a-blaze with the devil's music, even Ern's fiddle catching the tune when Maud got too near. If only the music could have been stopped altogether, but the pastor knew when not to go too far, and the few could do as they would, as long as the hearts were his. The souls were God's. But Maud, with her song, and Ern, with the tune, could set dead feet tapping, could make a corpse want to whirl around the floor. The music could hook the ears and tap feet that shouldn't be tapping. Her looks so soft sometimes, like oil on wool with oil on the hands, and it lit by kerosene light till it looked like the Golden Fleece. Lamplight somewhere in her eyes mixes with smoke, too.

When his thoughts had gone that far, he would pray for guidance, would let the bible fall open at random. His hand to the verse with his eyes closed, his other hand under the spine of the bible, broad enough a hand to hold the bible wide open. His finger would touch the verse.... Once it read, "A whore is a deep ditch and a strange woman is a narrow pit." All verses, even if less direct, could spin and the hate would be there for Maud, as much a part of the thought of her as the grain is in oak.

Vince is now, for him, an answer. There is right on his side. He is a man who thinks for himself. Now the pastor waits for Vince. Vince is like a Knight Templar. A Mason living the moment of waiting for the temple-plans. The wait is sweet and worth it.

"Pastor, I'm ready."

"Ay, Vince, you're sure you don't want t'do it all from here? You're welcome to stay."

" No, there – that's my home. First, the Skipper's, now mine, Pastor. She's in my house. Would you wait?"

"There's still the family pew, in church."

"There's still the family."

Together they move towards the truck. One of the pastor's sons is polishing up the car, and the pastor decides to take the truck. The one truck of the town. The cab is white and round like a bread roll before it's baked.

The suitcase is thrown in the metal pan, the pan pitted with marks of rocks and with small rust spots like freckles. The suitcase bounces and clangs against the tailgate. Vince and the pastor high in the seats, watch the town go by. Two children chase the truck but, seeing the look the pastor gives them, stop running and pretend to be looking for something on the road.

All along the road curtains are pulled back and blinds raised. Old men and old women watch. One or the other is to the side peering out and reporting to the other what is happening at the house of Ern. The first report has the pastor's truck pulling up at the fence. They've already seen Arnold come by carrying his suitcase, and then going inside after a long talk with Maud. So they know he was welcomed, or he would never have got inside the door. Now the pastor gets out and picks up the suitcase, and passes it to Vince. The two of them shake hands, and the pastor gets back in the cab. But instead of driving away he turns off the key, and settles down to watch what's happening. Vince shakes his head, and motions him away. The pastor starts the truck, and drives away watching the rear view mirror, 'til the dust fills where the speck of Vince was. Then the hill is in the way of the mirror. And back at the house, Vince arrives at the door.

He is reaching for the latch, when the door flies open to the outside, skinning his knuckles, so the suitcase is dropped. This is such a sudden, such an unexpected pain that his anger is quick and bitter, but more at the door than anything else. For this is different from anything that he could have imagined, and is a puzzle. And Maud is at the door, but she is looking stronger than he thought she could. He sucks at his skinned knuckles, the metal taste of blood on the tongue, and picks up his suitcase.

"What's the suitcase for, Vince?"

"What the hell do you think it's for. Got my stuff in it."

"If you want a cup of tea, or a bite to eat, you're welcome to it. But the suitcase stays outside."

"Not goddamn likely."

"No, b'y, this is Ern's house…and mine, and there's no jeezly way that you're bringin' a suitcase in. 'Cause Ern wouldn't let the likes of you stay in this house."

For Vince the world has stopped and is watching him. He knows the curtains are back from all the windows around the point. He knows that old women are calling old men to come and take a look. He is aware of his different-looking suit, the slope of his shoulders, the scuff of dirt to the side of the trousers, the suitcase huge as a boulder near him, and Maud blocking the way into the door. The pastor gone, he has hurt his hand, and the only way out doesn't offer much dignity.

He puts down the suitcase. His hand feels so light, it's going to fly up. Just like that trick where you stand in a doorway and press the back of each hand to the door jamb…full strength until you can't do more, then step forward and your hands fly up. And he walks past Maud into the kitchen and sees bold as brass Arnold sitting at the table with a hot mug of tea in his hand.

"What the hell is he doin' here?" Vince snaps a look-question at Maud.

"He asked…you didn't…."

"Arnold, you dumb son of a bitch. Get your suitcase and clear out."

Arnold doesn't move. He looks at his hands.

"It's time to go. See what she's trying to do, split us one from the other. Just the same as when the Skipper was alive."

Maud pauses by the stove. She takes the top off one of the pots, and steam drifts around her head until it's like a cloud is living on the top of her shoulders. Arnold is sipping tea, and pausing to break off little bits of bread from a crust that he spread with thick white butter.

Maud looks at Vince, and sets the lid back on the pot.

"Vince, b'y, it isn't the way it was when the Skipper was alive. He's dead. Ern is dead, Bessie is dead. And in this little house there is no room at all for horseshit. And that's what you always talked, and always will. But you're Ern's brother. Which is the best thing I can ever find to say about you. Have a mug of tea."

But Vince doesn't. He is in one move walking out of the house, the door left open. His anger is so great that he can't think of anything to say, anything to do. He has lost the thought of who might be seeing him, of who might think what about him, of Arnold, of the house, anything. He is so angry that he wants to cry, his collar is tight, and his chest is hot. His hands twitch with the shudder of anger. He strides to the suitcase lifting it on the strength pumping from his heart. All the world is rushing in his ears, his cheeks are so hot that the cool air is like the flame of ice candles touched to them. He is striding down the path. The hate is so that it fills his body.

When he stops, winded, he is half a mile down the road, the suitcase is heavy, and he knows he is being looked at. There is a horse with a load of longers towing behind it, and some old skipper on the front, walking along. He nods to Vince who gets on the load of sticks, and moves towards the pastor's house.

The wood smells of turpentine, the sap of burst bubbles leaking down to crystallized bits of dried tree blood. And all the smell holds him and comfort him. The ridges of the wood, the shift of them and having to shift himself to keep being pinched by the longers as they restless move to and fro. The horse lets out a giant fart, and the skipper turns windward and Vince laughs. The first time it seems to him in a year. And the horse and the load keep moving slower towards the arm, towards the pastor's house.

Chapter Twelve

Now Arnold is, for the first time in his life, startled as a cat. He is also very happy, and though he sits as still as he ever sat, his words tumble all around him.

"Maud, o my God, did you see his face? He were as red as beef. I thought he was gonna swell and bust. Bits of Vince all over the cove. I done it. I done it. That's the first time I ever done it. He always told me what to do, what I was s'posed to do. My Lord, I done it."

And Maud looks at him. Her smile hangs around her neck. Arnold's smile grows even bigger, and now he moves. He leaps to his feet, just missing putting his head through the ceiling, and begins to pace all around the kitchen. He is back and forth, he is skating on the diagonal, he is almost hop-scotching the linoleum. "What a happy round cat he is," thinks Maud and she laughs. Arnold joins in. The stove shines to their eyes. It shines with a black deep laugh, and the kettle shines a silver laugh. The old clock is ticking a laugh to the second. But deep down, Arnold is scared, and all the memories, half of a piece of the night memories flick at him.

In the memories Vince was near to him as Arnold danced around the yard on a new pair of stilts. His logans were loose on his feet and he could feel the new young wood press against the side of his feet. The feet of the stilts half stuck in the mud, and he kept a steady pace so the earth wouldn't grab them away. "Arnold, I wants they." No threat from Vince, not in that voice. There just was the sound of his knowing that soon he would be on the stilts. Vince was standing there, the rain fell adrift around his head as he waited for Arnold to get off the stilts. But that time Arnold didn't do what Vince expected him to. He shook his head and tipped further away.

Vince wanted no debate. He didn't look at all surprised. He looked like he was expecting some moment like this, and was ready for it. Without a word he moved towards Arnold, who loped away tipping to the side like a fat seagull. Round the garden they made wide and mud-sucked circles, faster and faster till Arnold was in his hurry passing close to Vince who without a rush, without a sign of anger reached out his hand as he bent over and taking the bottom of one stilt in his grip, pulled that stilt out from under Arnold.

Arnold has stopped pacing around the kitchen now. He goes back to the table and sits down as Maud watches him. In his mind he feels himself falling, floating from the stilt world.

He is conscious of the rain that dampened the wool of his shirt and breeches and wetted them to him, he is even now still conscious of the hurt of his foot as it twisted off the other stilt. As he hit in a squish with the feel of rocks cutting him 'til the mud oozes hurt his side, his back hurting as Vince knelt on him and pushed his face into the wet earth. Then Vince was gone, and Arnold scraped mud out of his eyes, he felt grit scratch his face as he wiped it off, and as he watched Vince, now on the stilts run crazy skidding circles into the mud. In all the wet and slippery earth, Vince never slipped, the circles tight and fast.

And Arnold looks at Maud. He thinks she looks tiny in the kitchen.

"He's after the house, Maud. He gotta have it."&&&

"Sure, I knows that, Arnold. But, 'tis mine. He can't have what's mine. See how simple things is?"

"Maud, I'm going home. I got to."

And Maud, without saying a word, nods her head. She goes over to Arnold and hugs him. He can feel her heart. Like being hugged by a loaf of bread, he thinks. He starts to cry, and then he starts to sob. But he doesn't care, not a bit, though he knows he should be mortified. Instead he cries, and Maud holds him. The light is lower in the day and dark is coming to the kitchen, and Arnold has sobs that are softer. It is almost full dark and Arnold stops his crying, and Maud takes her apron and wipes his face, she kisses him on the mouth. Arnold starts to kiss back when he realizes that all it is is a good-bye, and he stands back.

He turns towards the door. He doesn't know how to say anything more and he stops with his back towards Maud as she reaches towards Maud as she reaches towards the doorlatch. His back is saying it all. He hears the scrape of a match and the click of the lamp mantle being lifted. Light, wet and yellow, is licking his shoulders and he is almost washed back into the room, feeling like he is on stilts. He goes through the doorway, and into the dark of the yard. He sees his shadow before him. It is faint and it flickers. The door closes and his shadow has left. Cold is the night and it cups Arnold for a cold moment. His eyes start to adjust and he sees other small lights dot the cove. He figures out where Amador's house is, thinks of the boat that will take him away. Arnold wonders why his face feels gritty, and for a moment he looks back at the house.

The window holds Maud who looks straight at him. Arnold can't move and Maud slowly pulls down the blind. He turns away from her, and as he walks to leave the cove, he holds the window in his mind. It fades and Arnold walks faster. He is going home.

Chapter Thirteen

All the ride to the pastor's house Vince is thinking. At first his anger is as bitter as bile, he can taste it at the back of his throat wanting to make him cough. Later his thoughts are as clear as fall ice. His thoughts so clear and good that they carry him back into the pastor's house, they describe the events with a crystal logic to Pastor Roberts, they keep him all through the creaking night awake and planning.

When morning comes to the house he is relaxed. Vince now feels sleep moving closer. He lies under the huge quilt that checkers the bed, and is enclosed by the feather mattress. Sleep comes as the sounds of the kitchen drift to the bed. The muffled voices, the clanging echo of a lid being returned to the stove after the thuds of small wood being dropped in. Then the smells on the morning air, bread being toasted, strong tea steeping on the stove, bacon frying, and all mixed together in a smell so mingled and good that you could eat it.

Vince sleeps and the pastor thinks. He makes his morning prayers. To do this he takes out a small footstool and places it on the floor near a window that overlooks the cove.

He kneels on the stool, and laces his fingers together while looking out the window as he talks to God. The pastor does not close his eyes. It was his belief that the image of the world should not fade when he talked to God of a morning. He wanted to see the place where he had helped God overcome the sin of that day. He and God had joined forces to fight, and that alliance could never be shaken; that alliance was foretold. It was hinted at in small passages that smoked and rang like dream bells in the works of the Prophets. Pastor Roberts had to stand by the ocean, where the clouds rolled into shapes that

God patterned, the world rang with the fading echo, the fading sight of a moment where God had printed a picture of Himself so clear that if only mankind had not eaten the apple they could have gazed in delight, in a rapture that would never end. Instead Man and Woman together ate the apple and because of that the bridegroom rushed down the hall and down the hall and out the door leaving only a shadow held by the morning air. The pastor looked at his cove, looked at the houses where his people sinned. "How long, O Lord – how long, O Lord?"

And now the morning prayer is started, his voice through the walls rolls towards the kitchen and his family keeps quiet. They move like monks under the greatest vow of silence that could ever be made. They glide with plates of toast across the kitchen floor, they pour cups of tea and the tea splashes in the cups as though the cups are made of plaster-of-Paris cheesecloth. Everything in the house becomes still and through the walls rolls the pastor's voice.

"O, Lord, this is a morning of sin. You should see in the light of the morning your servants all along the streets, all on the very edge of the ocean, on their knees weeping for their sins – crying that their souls were lost and in peril of death, in peril of flames forever.

They need You to find forgiveness – to find salvation. Lord, there is a woman in this community who is a woman of sin.... Help me save her, help me crush the evil from her life...."

And the pastor prays. He watches the boats return from the morning's fishing, he watches how much fish is unloaded from each boat, keeping it in his memory like a nut. When it comes time to fill the collection plate for the glory of God, he will remember who has caught the most fish, he will remember every gutting. Sinners all, the fishermen laugh and joke and make the water run red and make the gulls circle and scream, make the women in their households of sin cook and ready the house, send the children of sin, the children of lust, all a-chatter in the morning air down to see their fathers land the fish. The knives slit the guts of the fish, steel glides through silver, pink on the inside, red the blood. Salmon and cod and the mackerel all at their own times bleed into the cove.... "To everything its season," thinks the pastor. "Make this my season of harvest, o Lord. Amen. Praise the Lord, Amen, forever. Amen, dear Lord, Amen."

And the pastor gets up from his prayers. His knees creak and he thinks of Peter's denial of Jesus three times, and all because of the body. The pastor decides to eat breakfast.

Holding to his prayer thoughts he speaks not to his family. They don't notice, used to his silence after his prayers, but they feel freed from the vow of silence and they prattle like jays to each other. They eat with such noise, the clacking of the teeth and the slurping of tea, to such a volume that if you were to stand outside the pastor's house you would guess that fifty people or more had jammed into the tiny kitchen and were eating, eating loud enough to make a deaf man leave the house.

The pastor stays, he thinks of Jesus, he thinks of his own trials and he plans out his Sunday sermon, he will take the Sabbath sun and he will roll it down the aisles 'til it catches the sinners on fire and in the flames of sin, of sin being burned, they will scream and run their lives into glory.

Breakfast is eaten, and all the family leaves the table. One plate covered with another stays on the back burner. Still in his dream of glory, the pastor picks up the plate, and now he eats, and sips his tea. O Lord, he thinks, it is a long voyage, and the waves are many, and they are strong!

Vince wakes up and listens to the house. What he hears more than anything is the voice of Ruth, daughter of the pastor. She is as sweet and dark and rich as molasses.

> *Forty years ago*
> *Forty years ago*
> *I loved to hear*
> *The preacher's voice*
> *Forty years ago.*

Vince knows the hymn and he joins in and as he sings along with Ruth he can feel their voices blending, his voice hard as flint covered away in the rich dark flow. The voice in the hallway hesitates and for one line Vince is singing alone and she has stopped. But Vince keeps on singing, 'til another line is sung, and slowly, her voice less sure, smaller and held back, she joins again. Through the wall they keeps singing and her voice is now stronger, and together they are singing the "Amen." For one moment Nelly slips through his mind. She is on skates and the snow is all around. Nelly falls, but Vince doesn't go over to help. So thin, she drifts to the ice and slides along it like a skate blade. The snow melts and Nelly is gone.

Vince looks around the room. He feels hot and the covers hold him and the voice of Ruth is sweet and warm. Vince hears her steps move along the corridor and towards her room; a door slams shut. Now he is awake. Now he is with the morning.

The pastor is back in his study. He has prayed. He has eaten. Now he is studying his plans. Later he will read the Holy Word. He listens to Ruth sing and smiles when he hears Vince join in. He unrolls his drawings and looks at them as sunlight pours over them.

The plans came to him in an early dark-time morning. He was dreaming. Having read from the Prophets the night before, Ezekiel burned in his mind like a chariot. In his dream he was with Ezekiel and rose through the clouds, even before the prophet; he rose as soon as the sky opened by that innocent and sleepy river bank. As the pastor flew through the sky he moved, his loins light as a cloud, towards a place so far away that it looked like the darkness of space. In the twinkle of a star he was there and there were paintings all over the clouds in pinks and purples and yellow as a buttercup with lines drawn as dark as the hardest coal. The paintings showed a tabernacle, the new tabernacle, and Christ himself was pointing at the drawings and flames leaped from his finger and the flame was blue and it burned out the black lines and it bounced and burned the plans of the drawings into the forehead of the pastor, and it burned him awake.

He was all of a sweat and his night clothes were the same as if he had fallen into the ocean. He leaped up and cold as the morning was, he strode through the house. It was a dark night, the moon was half hidden behind a dark smoke cloud but the steps of the pastor were certain, he could see the house as though it were full day. He walked to Ruth's room and opened the door. He went to her school bag and got out the paint set she had, and the pretty coloured pencils and now he knew why they had paints at school. He strode up the hallway. The winter air was freezing his garment to him, but he didn't feel it. In his study he lit the lamp and its light was to him so intense, a fireball that rolled like the wheel of a chariot, that he felt warm and with Christ in the cloud, and the blue flame was a resting place and it held his heart, o, it held his hand and his hand knew what he needed most. His hand was sure and the paints were right, and with his work he praised the Lord.

When that morning came and the winter light bounced in a white sheet through the room, the pastor knew it was a sign that his drawings had stopped. He looked at what he had drawn and knew deep in his heart that he had been given the plans to replace the old temple, that last shattered shell of lost hope.

He also knew that this place where he lived should always for history be called King's Cove, and that King's Cove was to be the building site for the temple. He told no one else this. The one thing he had not been told was where to build, where the Lord wanted his temple. But the pastor was willing to wait for his next dream. Each morning he would look at the plans, the drawings that he had done that dream morning, and although he was surprised the colours faded a little over the years and though he was startled that there was no mark on his forehead after his vision, he was never surprised that he was the person chosen for the message.

As he looks at the plans on this spring morning, and as summer moves closer to King's Cove, he watches the light melt along the paper, and he smiles. He doesn't hear the study door open and he doesn't hear Vince come into the room. Vince moves softly, Vince moves quietly and from behind the pastor he looks at the drawings.

Bessie had owned a book that she looked at often. The book has poems, the book had drawings all by someone called Blake. Vince had sneaked a look at that once just to find out what Bessie thought mattered. He spent most of the day looking at those drawings. So when he saw the pastor's drawings he knew what they were.

"Pastor?"

The pastor doesn't leap, he doesn't move, he knows that some day his drawings are meant to be seen. And he knows, in this moment, that the plans of his temple are meant to be seen by Vince.

Chapter Fourteen

Maud sleeps late this morning.

She awoke once at around four and reached for Ern, then she knew the where and the why of where she was and rolled over and drifted to sleep again. In her dream she was with Ern, the both of them in his dory and somehow the warmest kind of fog had put them in a grey mitten where they were held just on the line of sea and air. Neither one was rowing but slid along the water. Ern had his fiddle and played a soft slow kind of jig while the lines of the trawls cut the water as pretty, as quick and as quiet as butter. The music got louder and the boat started rolling. Gulls cut through the air and the distant sound of a fog horn rolled along the water. Maud was naked. Ern was in his long johns and they both started laughing. Ern stood on the gunwale of the boat as it tipped to one side. He played the fiddle and Maud smiled until, with a slip as sudden as plastic, he slipped into the water and still playing, drifted towards the bottom of the ocean. Maud looked at him as light poured from his fiddle and all the lines, the trawl lines, lit up in different colours like stained glass windows and fish all danced round Ern, round and round and all around the circle 'til Ern started, himself, to spin and in a great sweep and swirl of sand, a silicon vase of colour and light, he spun like a wet drill into the ocean's sand and the light blinked out and Maud was all alone and of a sudden the cold moved in and grabbed away the fog and there she was stark naked in the middle of George's Cove and everyone watching.

Now she's awake, and her head aches, and the blankets are on the floor and light is in the window. Maud wants to tell Ern the dream. She swallows the memories, and is down the stairs after her tinkle. She starts the pitch-filled fir burning in the stove and she watches the flames take the edges of the kindling; watches the brown edge run along the edge as the fire licks, and she puts the damper back on. She starts the water for her tea, and she singes some bologna and she cuts the bread for her toast. Maud does all that and never notices a thing she's doing. She looks out the window all the time seeing George's Cove and thinking of what it was without Ern, and why she was there.

She sits down and eats but she doesn't taste anything. It isn't so much the row that she's had and would continue to have with Vince, it is instead the dreary thought of living in a place where she isn't wanted. With Ern the only place that mattered was their own cove, the one they would have made anywhere that they were. The house was the house that it was because of Ern. Now she looks and the colour is washed out of it, leaving it as grey was a mackerel sky.

The taste of food comes back to her, and there she is – alone in her and Ern's kitchen. She cries a little, and then she does the dishes. After that she gets dressed putting on a nice green frock that Ern had always liked. She might be leaving, she would be leaving and she had a long way to travel, wherever she might be off to.

As she thought of leaving, she felt happier, the house felt warmer. Maud had not thought of leaving before. Always the house had seemed to her the centre of the world, everything else would have been a dream, a shadow on the water, a fish going by way down deep, a salmon, only the hint of a silver shine from some deep trapped sunbeam caught in a rock the half the depth of the ocean-bed. Up the net and no salmon, all that would be caught would be a rubbed scale off the side of the fish. The world that shimmered at the edges of her world was now right there in front of her.

She remembered that when she was a little girl they had a globe on the downstairs shelf. It was of cheap tin and bought second-hand. She wasn't supposed to touch it but she always did, and when she turned it, it always gave off a squeak enough to frighten her. But the sound never brought anyone, so she sat and turned the world, and watched the countries drift by floating in the blue. She would close her eyes and she would spin the creaky globe and put her finger on it and imagine herself in whatever place she could imagine. Because she knew every sound and every catching spot of the globe, she really could pick, even with her eyes closed, any place she wanted. Most times she'd end up in Africa, and would daydream herself into the desert. There she would be in the heat (a winter's day was the best day for the globe to land her there) and everything would shimmer like a lace curtain. She would have her favourite lion with her, and she would twine her little hand in the lion's mane and it would feel like unravelling marline twine, and rough and full of sand. She would scratch and the lion would purr.

Maud sits in the kitchen and she thinks about going to Africa. Perhaps she would find the desert. Even though she was grown up and not likely to find that kind of lion she could still take off her shoes and stockings, and feel the warm sand go rough between her toes. She could stand there wearing her green dress and feel the hot dry wind blow her dress between her legs and wrap her in cloth.

Perhaps she could get to Boston like Bessie had done. She smiles at that, because she knows that Africa would cost a lot more, and she really had no money. She and Ern had spent it as it came, every cent. Now there wasn't even the unemployment coming in from Ern's stamps. She had a little put by but that was going. Even if she wanted to leave she'd have to sell the house to get the money so either way, and she smiled, Vince was in trouble.

There was a point though, where money didn't mean anything. She had come to the cove with no money and she didn't mind leaving again without any. Come to it she could even do the same thing again – work in someone's house. Perhaps in Boston, perhaps in St. John's or in Toronto.

Maud looks around the little house, and thinks that all she'll take with her will be a couple of snapshots and Ern's old fiddle.

She wouldn't even tell Vince. She'd just pack her few clothes in the small grip, put on her green dress and head out.

She'd start up Ern's boat like she'd done a hundred times and then, in the night time, it being a clear one, take a fix on the stars over the point, put the distant light over the port bow and steam for down-the-coast, then sail the boat. Yeah. She could do that and then catch the coastal boat and that would be the last that George's Cove would ever see of her.

Or, an even better thought, that would be the last she'd ever see of the cove.

Chapter Fifteen

Spring has come to George's Cove. Now in the morning there's no skim of ice on the puddles, no steam off the hoar-frost as the tilted sun beams down on it. Instead, the day starts in a ball of warm sounds and smells that roll right in through the bedroom window. Maud stirs in bed and sniffs at the morning. She turns over on her side and sleeps. Through the window she hears the clang of the church bell and she pulls the covers firmly over her head.

The bell clatters its iron tongue over the churchyard and into the cove. Already small boys are standing around one side of the old graveyard, small girls whisper and giggle on the other side. Some adults are on their way up the crooked path that leads to the church.

The church is small and white as flour. The door is painted a strong green, the same shade that's used on a lot of the boats that bob at their Sunday moorings in the cove. In front of the church, bisected by a path rich in the crunch of bleached shells, there stands the graveyard. For the older members of the congregation, each Sunday is a walk past friends. It's also a small surge of triumph that they are the ones doing the walking. Some of the headstones have been made of marble. More of granite and a scattered few of crumbling, bleached ones and even the marble now holds faded letters. The graveyard is full and this, for the children, is a relief. Whenever they talk of death (and at the end of each Sunday service they do) they talk about how the view is better in the new graveyard. The older people would prefer to be amongst friends instead of being planted with the new generation, but as they say to one another, "You can't have everything."

Now there is a stirring outside the church, and an old man comes out and herds the children inside. The bell gives a few more clangs and then a kind of double clatter and stops.

Inside the church, in the murmur of voices, and the shuffling of feet, the last echo of the bell signals a quiet. As all the talk stops there is only the occasional cough and clearing of a throat. The sounds of the spring day drift into the church. A distant baaaa of new lambs bleats its way around the windows and the odd moo from Amador's famous milk cow presses against the pane. Most of the children have been placed in the middle of pews, squeezed between parents, or grandparents. However some lucky children, the first in through the church doors, have managed to keep a seat near the windows.

They sneak glances outside, and o, how green the grass is looking, and o, how sweet the sun upon the water, and every small boat a-dance. One small boy has not only managed to find a window seat on the pew, but he's also smuggled in a fragment of a pocket mirror. Children try to keep from giggling as the light plays around the bald knobbled head of old Joseph, the father of Amador. Some adults notice the light and they start to crane around trying to spot the guilty party. The reflection, that moment of sun on the mirror, vanishes as quickly as it arrived and the adults look back to the front. Every child's face looks as innocent as a daisy.

Now, of a sudden, the back doors swing open and the pastor walks in. He is followed by his family, and by Vince. Together they walk towards the pulpit. Vince is sombre and neat in a black suit that drifts mothballs across the children's noses. He sits with Ruth as the rest of the family goes to the choir section.

The three sons walk as a unit, almost as if they are welded together. Two pick up accordions, another picks up a tambourine. The wife of the pastor goes over to the pump organ. She rolls up the cover and the creaks echo round the church. The pastor opens his bible and Vince looks out of the corner of his eye at the way the sunbeams play over Ruth's face. They catch the curve of her cheek and play soft upon her lips. As Vince watches the play of the light, Ruth licks her tongue swift and wet along the length of her lips and the sun glints a slippery shine.

Suddenly all the accordions rip into the hymn, the tambourine rattles, the pump organ pumps, and the pastor rocks on the line of music. It's the old "One Hundred" and everyone leans into the words. The pace picks up, and the words are sung loud and sure. The windows rattle, and the outside sounds vanish.

Vince sings as loud as he's ever sung, and still through his own voice he hears the alto of Ruth, as clean and pure as a saw blade, tickle his ears.

The hymn is over, and everyone still remains standing. Now everyone in the church links hands, across pews, over aisles, back-to-front a lace of fingers linking everyone in the church. The pastor and his family all holding one another's hands, and the pastor leaning down towards Vince, and gripping his hand. Vince behind him, holds the hand of Ruth. And the pastor prays.... "O Lord, we are here in sin, burned by the fire of the devil."

AMEN.

"His breath is of smoke and sulphur and of a pool of brimstone, as wide as the ocean, as hot as the heart of coal!"

AMEN. AMEN.

Vince feels Ruth's hand, as hot as the heart of coal just mentioned and, hardly daring, he increases the pressure, just a touch, just a breath. And as quick as his breath can breathe back, as quick as one breath behind the other on a summer's day, she squeezes back. But that could have been an accident, and Vince squeezes harder. Ruth squeezes back as hard again and adding nails. They bite at Vince's hand.

The pastor rocks back and forth, his voice deep and ringing.

"Today, o Lord, we pour water on the fire, we steam holy thoughts in the very nose of the devil. We find out where lives the flame of Beelzebub, and we hold from it the air of life, until, blue of face, and with lungs burning, he dies!"

AMEN. PRAISE HIS HOLY NAME. AMEN. AMEN.

And the accordions start again, and the singing rocks the church, and the windows rattle even more, and Vince, his heart as hot as a coal, looks at nail prints in his hand.

The rest of the service, until the sermon, is a hot daze for Vince. Ruth has moved closer and he can sense her thigh and its pressure against his own. She is pressing her legs together and relaxing them with a slow steady rhythm and Vince tries to think of cold water. He bites the inside of his cheeks and he drives his own nails into his palms. But he cannot stop thinking of Ruth, and he dares to look at her. Her face is innocent, and in her eyes he can see only the light of the sermon. Vince wonders if all he thinks is happening is only in his own head. He focuses on the sermon. He listens as if he were the pastor's child himself. Now the blur of words clears up and Vince forgets Ruth. He forgets everything except the words.

"From this day on," says the pastor, "we are to be known only by the power of His name of the King of Kings – we are to be Kings, and I am to be the King's representative on earth. I will tell you of the splendour of His holy palace. To help us always think of His throne of sunlight, of the clouds that pour liquid marble at His feet, we are no longer George's Cove. Today we are King's Cove!"

AMEN. PRAISE THE LORD.

"Praise the King of Kings!"

PRAISE THE KING...

"Our king..."

OF KINGS!

"Of Kings!"

PRAISE THE KING OF KINGS!

"Amen!"

AMEN. AMEN. AMEN. AMEN. AMEN. AMEN. AMENENENENENEN.

And everyone is standing, and the hands are linked, and the music is playing, and everyone hugs everyone else and Vince and Ruth are close and Vince is hot and feeling the nearness of her and everyone in the congregation is swaying and then the music stops and the pastor stops talking and the swaying slows and the hands unclasp, and they look to the pastor. His hands are apart as they stretch out over their heads, and they bow their heads while he prays. He tells them of the fire of the devil, and of the heat that lives in the heart. Then the whole congregation breathes as one and their hearts beat as one, and everyone has the blood of fear beat against the fish gut inner skin of the inner ear, and they are all fearful that they are to be named, that they will be the one to have the SILENCE named against them. Just as the pastor is about to name the name, all hearts stop. In that silence, the quiet between the blood-beat, the pastor speaks the name of MAUD. And hearts beat again, and the music starts again, and everyone thinks 'Maud', and everyone knows that Vince will have the house again. And all know what they must do. Even the children know and together through the music, through the singing, after the last prayer, and while they walk home past the small graveyard they all think of one person – MAUD.

Chapter Sixteen

Maud wakes up to sunshine, and the smell of spring but she notices neither. Her thoughts are only about leaving and what she should take with her. After thinking about it for a while she decides on the fiddle. Everything else can stay and gather cobwebs for Vince. Now that she plans to give up the house she hardly notices a detail of it. She goes about making breakfast as if she's in the deepest of deep sleeps, so far down into the swirl of it that nothing else matters. The breakfast has no taste, the cleaning up after has no feel, and even going out into the finest morning that has ever rolled around two days in a row does nothing to touch her.

And so when it starts, at first Maud doesn't even know it's happening. She nods to Maisie in the house next door and doesn't notice that Maisie doesn't nod back, Maud doesn't even notice that the old woman hanging clothes to the line, in the small green house's back yard that she passes each morning, turn to her the broad of her back, and leaving the basket of clothes where it sits, go back into the small green house until Maud has passed by.

It's not 'til she's in the middle of a bunch of children that she notices something is wrong. The noises, the squeals, the laughter that always mixes in with the dust from the road and surrounds her like a cloud, doesn't happen. Instead the children become as quiet as they can be. Every laugh is cut in the middle as clean and as quick as scissors. The circles that dust King William are stopped before they join, and two little girls put their thumbs in their mouths before Maud's startled glance. This makes her look and this brings to her the morning with all its sun and warmth and Maud is alone standing in the road, alone in the centre of children who look neither at her nor away. "Now," thinks Maud, "something has happened."

She looks at the small boys.

"Is there anyone here," she wants to know, "as would like for me to show them how to make a whistle?"

It's spring, so the boys should be in the woods cutting alder trees for the whistles hidden in the branches.

"O," said Ern to a small boy once upon a few years back, "this is the way you does it. Don't pick out a crooked branch. Pick a section that's on a straight bit. There, that's the kind that Maud would pick."

"But she's a woman," said the little boy.

"What's that got to do with it? Maud makes the best whistles in the world."

The little boy didn't believe Ern and none of his friends believed him at all.

Ern's short fingers would cut two circles round the bit of branch, then make clean cuts around each end. Then you had a full tube of tree branch. Because the sap was running in between the wood and the bark, when you started with twisting motions the rind would slip off. When that was done the wood was sweet and when you bit it like you always did, then you'd find the taste bitter and green. Then you would carve with your IXL knife a sloping half section at the end and slip the bark back on, then notch above the slotted wood, and, o, what a whistle you had.

The whistle would be sharp, a shrill that mothers hated, that sang the bitter taste of wood across the water, clear to the other side of the cove.

They would be proud of their whistles. Proud until they heard the whistle that Maud had made.

Maud would always finish making her whistle and then put it in her pocket and walk on the path towards the wharves. The boys, seeing only a woman, would wait until she had passed by and then they'd blow the sharpness of their whistles on her.

She'd turn around in a motion so quick that the front of her skirt was still behind her, and blow her whistle back at them. And, o, the sharpness of what she carved – always it would be as loud as all their whistles blown together. And always they'd laugh and laugh and crowd round Maud till she showed them her trick in notching whistles. Then they would rush at alder trees and do the notch like she had shown them.

But this year they aren't going to ask.

This year they're scared that one of their mothers will see them with Maud. If that happens, they know that late at night they'll be crying in pillows and will feel the leather left in the welts that their father will give them.

But even in the quietness as they look away from Maud they hear the whistle she can make, and they dream of making the same sound.

Maud looks at them and she knows what has happened.

She knows that the silence has been called and that she has been named.

As she goes towards Billy Joe's store she watches the signs. In some house the curtains suddenly fall back as she looks towards them. In other windows the Venetian blinds rattle as her gaze shifts towards them. A couple of women cross to the other side of the road and find things to do that keep them from looking her way. Everything becomes real quiet and the distant sound of the last one-lungers coughing their way over the waves drifts into the street. The engines putt and putt and houses catch the echoes and roll them back at the sea and Maud looks as if her eyes are leaving the dream that would not leave her. Now the morning is as real as it could be and not a sound, a scent, or one shift of sun and shadow escapes Maud.

Two dogs sleep by the doorway to Billy Joe's. One of them wakes and knowing nothing of how he's supposed to feel about Maud, he wags his tail and makes a small bark welcoming her. She gives him a pat on the head and opens the door. When she goes in, the small bell over the door rings. This tiny sound drains every other in the store. Everyone looks at her and then away. Amador has just finished buying some Red Chief 'baccy and he walks with it held tightly in his hand. He walks past Maud, and tries not to look at her.

"Morning, Amador. Fine one, isn't it?"

He hesitates, about to speak then he speeds up and out of the store giving the door a mighty slam on his way out.

Maud is by the counter.

"Morning, Billy Joe. How's everything?"

He doesn't answer. He reaches over his head and with a quick flick of the hand snaps off half a fathom of twine, and looks at it as he winds it. He doesn't look at Maud.

"Got a sore throat? Don't worry, I'm not gonna try and get you to talk to me. I'm not even gonna take up much of your time. Just give us a bucket of salt beef. I'd like it delivered this afternoon."

He shakes his head.

"You ain't got none?"

He nods.

"You won't carry it over? Then I'll carry it myself. All you got to do is sell it to me."

He shakes his head. Maud looks right at him for a moment. He keeps looking at the twine and everyone in the store has eyes fixed only on Billy Joe. Maud, soft as a breeze shows no anger. She leaves the store and the bell rings out on the spring-time air.

Chapter Seventeen

Now it is night in George's Cove. The moon is out full, and only a few clouds are scudding across its face.

A scattered dog barks and a few more howl, but only every few minutes. The night is quiet and down at all the stage heads there is only the sound of the water round the pilings. Some of the boats that haven't been moored properly are rubbing wood to wood, with an intermittent squeaking. The wind isn't up much, just enough to whine a little at the corner of Ern's stage.

Inside, Maud sits and listens to all the sounds. The smell of the nets surrounds her and all about her is wrapped Ern's life. In the centre of the room there is a small pot-bellied stove and the glow from it goes orange and yellow on a bounce across the rough wooden floorboards. Through the open grate, bars of fire dance and Maud creaks open the door and puts in a few more small birch junks. As the door is opened a wave of heat splashes Maud and the room, and she leaves the door open and leans on the heat. She looks around the shed and sees Ern everywhere she looks. All the nets are stored as neat as a pin and according to mesh. One net is still hanging and the wooden needle next to it ready to complete the mending that Ern never finished. Each shelf holds small Mason jars and each jar holds sized nails and screws. The lids of the jars are screwed to the shelf board above them all as neat as can be. If you wanted just the right nail all you had to do was glance at the jar and then unscrew it, and put it back right after using it. On one wall all the shapes of the different tools had been painted and every tool was put in its place.

Over in the far corner lit by moonlight and firelight was a model schooner that Ern hadn't finished rigging. Maud looked at the small boat. The light threw the masts in shadow hard against the wall where, when they hot, they shimmered and shifted as if they were lying on the water.

"O, Ern, what am I s'posed to do?"

And Maud looks at the shadows as if they should form the letters of an answer. She cocks her ear and listens to the tiny catch of the wind on the building's edge, and the whimper of the waves of a new tide. She listens as though there's going to be the sound of Ern's voice. But there isn't an answer.

Maud sniffs the air. She looks in the corners and seeing nothing there, clangs the stove's door shut. The shadows leap at her and she lets them fold all round her like a shawl.

Now the net holds black patches of night time caught as quickly as a salmon, and wriggling like a smelt. As she looks at the net Maud starts to smile.

She moves closer. Now she picks up the awl, and she begins the quick stitch, and with the steady sweep of her arm she works faster and faster. She wants to repair the net by morning. As she stitches she looks through the net and over at the far wall where she sees Ern's Sou'wester and Cape Ann hanging on a hook and, underneath, his fishing boots.

The stove crackles a spit of flame as a birch junk shifts place and the heat grows for a minute. Maud listens and as she works she sings a small song to herself. This song has no tune and the rhythm changes according to the pace of her sewing. The words go to the knotting of the net. The light slips along the wall. More wood shifts and the light slides over some hand-made jiggers, squid with little red bug eyes, staring at the front of a hand-made fiddle as clean and new as pine when it's first cut.

"O, they thinks they're gonna take it," she sings.

Stroke of the arm, catch of the wind, whir of the twine.

"O, they thinks they're gonna own it. Send me home where I won't go. No, I won't go."

The shadows of the schooner drift along the wall, it sails as silent as fog, as huge as the way the water cups the moon.

"Ern, Ern, I misses you. Ern, Ern, I misses you."

And the fire dies down, and the shadow stops sailing, and the last dog is curled in the fur of sleep, and even the wind stops, and the moon fades, and the clouds stop scudding and join up, and all of the cove feels the first shift of the sun as it moves towards the almost morning. Maud has fixed the net, and Maud has stopped her song.

The silence has changed her mind – the silence has made her house her own.

Chapter Eighteen

Time has hooked between the morning and the curved moon. The wharf glows with silver and green. Amador smokes and the curl of smoke from the cigarette catches the orange colour as the sun slides closer. He flicks the butt away from him and watches it curve towards the water. Like someone spitting it hits and black rushes in to fill the dot of light.

Obadiah finishes loading the gear and waits for Amador who now walks towards the boat, his rubber boots slapping against the back of his legs. The worsted socks hold away the chill that frosts the black runner.

Near them old Abe Cootes is bailing out the rainwater from overnight. At least that's what he calls it. Though the rain hasn't swung towards the cove for almost a week. He'd never say the caulking wasn't done proper. Neither would anyone else.

The wooden scoop hits and scrapes the planks and the bounce is followed by a splash into the water. Pipe pumps are clanging away and the wood on pipe clinks away as well. Amador drags another net towards the boat and Obadiah rolls a smoke as he smiles.

"My God, you're not putting out another net, Amador?"

"Why not? All the fishes have passed on the word 'bout where the other ones is. Not a fin scraped by any of them. Word mightn't get out for a while 'bout this one."

"They musta told about mine, too."

Amador smiles back.

"I'm hopin' this one'll fool them, gonna use Ern's old berth near the point."

There is a moment when the talking stops, and the pumping and the splashing and echoes all cease. There isn't a fisherman on the wharf who hadn't wanted to take over Ern's berth. It was a sweet one and had been in the family for as long as anyone could remember. Other coves might draw for their berths – but here they were passed down as secure and as placid as a pew.

The only question as far as anyone was concerned was what Vince would do about the berth. Most people thought if he wasn't going to use it he should put it up for grabs. Maybe then they could have a draw for it. Some of the younger fellows, especially those who had inherited a mean scummy kind of berth, thought all things should be done that way. After the silence that follows his remark, there's a chorus of cries at first from the younger crowd but then from the elders as well condemning Amador. All that is left after a while is one comment, that comes from near about everyone – the idea that Vince should decide. Amador looks around and what he sees is anger. The early light now shows flushed faces, necks that strain with cords, and even Obadiah looking stern and angry. So Amador backs down.

He walks back to the stage with the net, and stops. He stops as sudden as a gull. For there is Maud. She is wearing Ern's oilskins. She is carrying the twine net she's mended. She walks past Amador and not a word is spoken to anyone.

In complete silence she moves towards Ern's boat – the *Maud & Me*, a thirty foot skiff. It's trimmed with light green around the gunwales. The rest is painted as white as white can be. A green diamond is painted on the engine hatch. Still holding the net Maud jumps, sure-footed, from the wharf to the gunwale. She walks the length of it shifting her balance as she goes. The boat tips and bobs till she jumps down. She sets down the net and slides up the hatch cover. The engine looks as clean as a clock. She looks up at Amador's outraged face.

"You cast down the painter f'r me, Amador? No need to answer that if you'm taken the vow of silence."

"T'hell with that. You plannin' on usin Ern's berth?"

And everyone waits for the answer. Maud looks back at the engine. She starts to prime it. Then she looks back where Amador and the world are waiting for the answer.

"Yes, Amador, I am."

"Goddamn it, Maud, I was planning to use the one by the point!"

"It isn't yours to plan to use."

"We all agreed that we'd ask Vince and draw for it."

"It isn't Vince's to ask about. It was Ern's, now 'tis mine. That and the house and the boat."

Now Obadiah is on the wharf. His question reaches Maud before he does.

"Who said you could use the berth?"

"Anyone here live with Ern longer? He love anyone of the whole lot of you, you bloody sculpin faces? Ern! He's the one says I can use whatever the hell I want. Amador, I asked you to cast off the painter."

Amador, without looking away from Maud, reaches into his pocket and takes out the clasp knife. He cuts through the painter and the boat starts to drift away. The wind and the tide and the moon suck the boat away from the pilings. Maud doesn't drop her look from the eyes of Amador. She doesn't look to see where the boat drifts.

"One person can do this work if I got to."

"One man might. You'm a woman, that's the difference."

"I don't care if I'm a tom cod, I knows how to fish. You'd have cast off the painter for Ern."

"I s'pose we would. He was a man."

"That makes him a lot different from the rest of you lot, then."

And Maud looks away. She takes the piece of wood that Ern carved out of good solid plank, and puts it in the flywheel. She gives it an almighty heave and nothing happens.

Again she gives it another heave as now the *Maud & Me* drifts towards the rocks on the other side of the cove. She spins it again and the one-lunger catches. It coughs and spits out a cloud of oil-filled smoke, and the exhaust pipe trembles as the catch holds and the sound reverberates from the three walls of the cove. The smoke comes in clouds and then settles into a stream and Maud grabs the tiller as the skiff gains momentum and she skims past two other boats.

Now she goes past the sunkers and she's near the capehead. The wind and the smell of salt are all mixed together with the odour of oil and exhaust, and she can almost smell the way it was when she was a little girl on her father's boat. She tiny and scared of whales. Once she'd seen a picture from a book of a whale with a small boat all crunched and planks a-rib on top of it. She was always scared when she was a little girl and she is scared now. But not of whales. The anger has left her and she is all alone on a sea that's getting better every second she's on it.

She looks back at the cove so tiny, the wind on the back of her head and the smoke in a stream, and she sees her house. It catches on its windows the first angled rays of the sun and it beams them right back at Maud as shiny as a salmon's scale and the bounce of it on the water cheers Maud's heart.

Maud is no longer scared. She listens to the engine as true as her heart beat. She sees some other tiny chips of boats sprinkled out of the cove. She looks away and towards Ern's berth. "No," she thinks, "towards my berth." There are the little flags and she looks forward to the day. She remembers what Ern always said about this early of the morning, this sound of the engine and smell of oil and salt.

He'd look at her and the wind would wet his eyes.

"O, Maud, isn't this as good as your breakfast?

Now she says to the wind, to the gulls that follow the boat, to the rocks that get closer, and the scrub trees that dip away from the water, "O, yes. My God it is."

Chapter Nineteen

The sound of the small boats drifts into the house of the pastor. It mixes with sounds from the bluebottle fly that buzzes, butting its head against the glass. The clock ticks and a kettle sings from the distant kitchen.

Light wipes the pastor's window. It splashes on the floor of the study. Two slanted rays light up a model of the dream tabernacle. Already it holds the shape of what the pastor's head held before only in his mind or slipping out of the pencils colour. Vince is helping. Both look at the wild drawing as though they're studying a blueprint of the Brooklyn Bridge. Neither speaks.

With a gesture that seems so slow as to be underwater the pastor mixes an intense blue paint. The robes of the prophet, the robes of the wise men might have held such blue he thinks. He mixes and watches the different levels of blue. Some are like the sky, some are like the edge of a lake, still more like the blue hidden away in a log fire. As pure as a child's eyes.

Vince watches the blue. He is not a spiritual man but he has caught some of the pastor's mad spirit and though he started with the project to win the pastor, now he wants to see the house of God rise from the ground like it's rising from the table under the steady and frantic hands of the pastor.

The door opens and neither looks up. Ruth sets down the tea things and moves away towards the curtains. Now she leans back and folds of the curtains slip around her; she feels the touch of the velvet even through her clothes. Vince looks up and he sees her eyes. They blaze with a blue that not even the paint may catch, they blaze in blue to his whole body and he feels a flush of fire tingle its way through him. The pastor dips the brush and smears paint onto the model. The blue licks along the roof and drips off the eaves. Ruth smiles at Vince.

She turns and goes. For a long time Vince doesn't move. When he does look down it's at the wet paint. The sun glints off it and blue fire runs along the drops. Vince thinks of Ruth and her eyes. He picks up another brush and he and the pastor paint the tabernacle. It shines in the day's clear sun.

In the afternoon Maud sleeps on Pilly's Island. Her boat is moored near the beach. She lies on a bank of moss deep in the woods there. Her head is against a tree hung with the green-grey folds of molldow. Some has tangled with her hair and every time she moves the tree seems to sigh and move with her. Leaves lie under her. They fell so long ago that they don't make any noise even when she moves.

The forest is quiet. As silent as a glass of water and as still. Light slips around the trees and slides down the bank of a small stream. The stream is clear and all the rocks hold small mantles of green. A bird chirps and Maud awakens. For a moment she does not know where she is and she sits up so quickly that her head feels giddy. The trees sway and criss-cross on a net of light. A bird flying from the branch is a tissue in the wind. Noise comes back and the wind, for the first time since she fell asleep, moans round the trees at the edge of the forest. The noise reaches Maud slowly – it moves like a furry tiny forest creature. But it is enough. She stands up, and begins to put on her oilskins again. The heat of the day makes them smell of tar. She tips a little and catches herself on a nearby tree.

The tea in the pastor's study has gone stone cold but he pours anyway. His eyes are empty and drained of dreams. He pours with automatic hand and the tea as strong as birch bark splashes into the white cups. His eyes are empty and full of dreams. Sleep moves into them and a bedroom warm-under-the-sheets look drifts along them like a boat with a filling sail.

They both turn to look at the model. Crimson and green and gold and blue is caught like a rainbow trout on ice. Both look. Slowly the pastor drinks. Slowly Vince watches him.

On the ocean a small boat bobs its way along the net. Maud is leaning over the gunwales as hand over hand she is towing the boat the length of the net. The oilskins catch and roast the heat and all is black tar and heat. In the water her arms are like the ice. They hold every blue and green and black of the water. They chill in silver flashes that make her stop. Like a spinning coin arcing its spiral through the water, light is caught and spills upward. Maud pulls up the net and tips the fish into the boat. They thrash and tail-to-head make loops around the boat. She does not let them lie. She does not let them batter their way around the planks. As quick as quick can be she with the knife is to their throat. Their muscle is against her hand and pulses away. At first slippery the scales leave glue along her hand. She cuts and the blood is shifting out along the knife. They bleed onto the planks and are still. She finishes bleeding all the fish and with the wooden bucket rinses salt along the salt. A tarp covers the still mound of pink and silver and she starts the engine.

Tomorrow she'll switch the net again. Today shows a good catch.

The sun is cool upon her face.

The sun is hot along the brow of Vince.

The sky for both is blue.

Chapter Twenty

Now the smell of fish and salt is as white as the aprons of the widows. Flies buzz and blend with the sounds of boats crossing the cove.

Sue stands next to Maud while the rest of the women stand away from them, The two work as if they were one person with four hands. All is attention to the turning and curing of the fish. The other women talk but not to Maud or to Sue. They talk in low buzzing murmurs – until the wind shifts around a few points. Then every word is carried on a platter to Maud. Each word rests there long enough for her to stare at.

Maud is wearing an old faded pair of green work trousers that used to belong to Ern. Tar stains are all down the front, and one leg has white paint stuck to it. She wears a checked black and green flannel shirt. It's too big for her and the wind blows the shirt tails of it around her waist. The legs of the trousers wrap around her legs and make them stand out like they belonged to a gull. Sue is wearing an old yellow coat that's faded like a piss-a-bed after the frost. She has on an antique knotted cap that hugs her hair despite the heat.

They work and the words go all around them.

"She'll move. Fishin' indeed."

"She caught more fish than half the men together!"

"It still be wrong. It be man's work and that's that."

"Evil is as evil does."

"Amen."

For a while Maud and Sue pay no attention. They brush the words off to the side the same way they flick away the flies. But just like the bluebottles the words come back to

Maud and to Sue as if the two women were made of honey and molasses.

Maud turns right to the women and talks to them over the words.

" 'Lo, Gert. 'Lo Sarah. Careful the sun don't cure you. Wonderful grand day, isn't it? No words? You was all talkin' up a storm a minute ago. Cat got your tongue? Sue, I 'lows that must be it. Listen to the wind – no more words."

Sue keeps right on turning the fish. But for a second she stops and cocks her head, then she shakes it to tell Maud, no, she doesn't hear a word. Maud doesn't let up as she flings a few more words against the wind.

"At least this be proper woman's work. Needs a lot of concentration for it, keep you happy. Perhaps we should all sing a hymn together. 'In the Sweet By and By'. That's be just the thing."

And Maud starts right in. She's back to the work but now every move is to the rhythm of the hymn.

In the sweet by and by.

She bundles up the first cured fish.

We shall meet on that beautiful shore.

And the voices of the women start up again but to each other and if Maud hears something the words aren't spoken to her.

"Now do you see why 'tis evil?"

"Why?"

And Maud sings *In the sweet by and by.*

"You need to ask that?"

Again her voice strong: *We shall meet on that beautiful shore.*

"Next thing you'll be getting' on the wrong side of the preacher."

"For thinking?"

Maud's voice echoes around the cove.

There's a land that is fairer than day
And by faith we can see it afar
For the Father waits over the way
To prepare us a dwelling place there.

And now Maud is flying at the fish. Every move is a note and her work is catching sunlight and all the words bounce off her as she moves, and Sue is tired but she still keeps time 'til they finish the work. They keep singing and together they leave the fish flakes taking care to tread careful where some of the longers are rotted and moved apart.

Maud thinks of her great-grandmother and the dream she had of falling and, in the song, the sun and the work all become one, and as she sings the hymn she sees Ern. He is this time playing the saw and it is telling her of the sweet by & by and in every word with every chord she sees Ern singing. The river is the river Jordan and it is a sandy bank that runs in a great swirl down to the clearest cleanest river you could ever hope to see. People are all sitting along its banks. Some people have been there a long time and are wearing clothes out of a dim and distant past. Others are naked and splash in the water. Ern has on the clothes he wore on the day he was took which Maud thought was odd because she had expected him to be in the clothes he was dressed in the day he was buried. He still has the saw and on it he plays *"In the Sweet By and By."* Maud joins in and Ern looks up to see her and she smiles at him and he back at her. And Maud hears Sue, and wonders how she got there. Sue's yellow coat is a blaze like a butterfly on fire. "Maud," she is saying, "Maud!"

The hymn stops and Maud blinks the world back around her.

She is standing on the dirt path outside her house and Sue looking at her like she had sunstroke, and asking again and again how she is. It takes Maud the longest time to persuade Sue that she is just fine, and finally Sue says good-bye and Maud watches her go. As she looks towards her friend she sees the coat of Sue catch the sun and roll it around and the yellow blazes again so fierce that she has to look away. She wants to call out Sue's name to warn her but thinks Maud, "What should I warn her about?" But before she can call out Sue has vanished. Maud's eyes hurt and she goes inside. The door creaks and slams and all Maud can hear is the hymn. She takes down the fiddle, she tunes it and she scratches out the melody.

That night she scratches the song out one more time. Then to bed. She blows out the lamp, but not without looking at it just before she does. So even when the light goes out she holds in her eyes a cloud of light all purple and ringed with gold. As the cloud fades Maud sleeps.

The cove sleeps.

Moonlight slips along the water and catches on the waves. It holds a shadow against the 'Maud & Me'. It shatters on the flakes, and bits of it lie on the rat trails. In Maud's kitchen it licks the strings of Ern's fiddle.

The cove dreams.

Amador is on a wide sandy beach. The beach has one palm tree. A woman in a grass skirt is swaying as he sings and plays his guitar. She is as brown as a tatey skin. She shines like cod liver oil. She looks at him and all she says is his name. She says it while the waves join Amador's song, and the wind whistles through his strings and around his heart.

The wife of Amador dreams. She dreams of the winter and its fierce heart. She dreams she is inside a Christmas dome. It has one small tree and a little house with yellow light that falls along the snow.

She smiles and the whole world turns upside down and her skirts fly up over her head and the snow drifts by. The snow is wet and warm and lies on her skin. The wind blows through the snow and around her heart.

Obadiah dreams.

In the distance he sees Maud standing in the middle of a crowd of boys. His two sons are standing there with the rest of the boys. All of them float above the ground and drift and bob like gulls in the swell. She has made a whistle and she plays it. As she plays she rises higher and higher until all the sons drift after her. His sons follow the whistle and they all drift into the forest like snow flakes.

The whistle tickles Obadiah's ribs, it blows a wind around his heart.

Maud sleeps.

She dreams again of the river. She feels the heat of the sand, she feels the water's coolness as cold as the first snow. As welcome to the eyes as if she was a child again.

"In the Sweet By and By" and she melts into Ern, both of them the one. His song is all around her and Ern has drifted like sand around her heart.

She dreams.

At first all is dark and she is scared. Then a small light glows and behind it she hears singing.

Sue sings.

"We shall sing on that beautiful shore

The melodious songs of the blest
And our spirits shall sorrow no more
Not a sigh for the blessing of rest."

And as she sings Sue goes behind the light and she sees a river. The sand sweeps down to the water and all along the shore are people in all kinds of dress. Some are naked and in the water, Ern is there and he plays the saw. Sue smiles and the music is all around her and whistles through her heart. Her yellow coat blazes and is as sweet as the sun.

Maud wakes up.

The night is cold and the moon even colder. In the light that holds shadows to her face she is crying and she doesn't know why.

She weeps and the tears are warm. As they run down her cheeks they get colder and colder. She licks the tears and they are salty, they taste bitter.

Chapter Twenty-One

Sue is dead. Her soul like an old gull flew into the sun until it became the sun.

Sue is dead and Maud is looking to her funeral.

When she went to Sue's house in the morning – the early of morning the fishing time – she thought before she got there that Sue was dead. Nothing was a surprise. Not even when she opened the door and found no fire in the stove and the kitchen dead and cold. Nor when she climbed the stairs every step a shout of floor boards and still Sue did not answer. When she opened the door to the bedroom of Sue, she saw her folded into the arms of the feathers.

None of that was a surprise.

What was a surprise was the smile on Sue's face. It still held there though the skin had gone stiff and yellow. Every hair on her head stood out in relief, and her arms were folded like a sparrow's wings.

Her smile still shone and her open eyes caught the light. Maud closed Sue's eyes and did what had to be done.

When she had finished cleaning the body and dressing it she went back to her own house. Before she went in she washed her hands at the pump outside her house. She dressed herself in her best and went to look after the funeral.

Maud stands now outside the pastor's house. For a moment she hesitates before she knocks and listens. She can hear Vince and the pastor talking but she can't hear what they are saying. She can hear the radio on – tuned to a gospel station. There is no music just the sound of someone praying. In another room she can hear the brothers playing a hymn. She hears a kettle whistle on the stove.

She knocks on the door. The sound of her knocking finds its own way into the house and echoes back to the ears of Maud. The echo is followed by Ruth who flings open the door. For a moment Maud is startled. It seems to her that she herself has answered the door. Ruth looks so much like the way Maud felt when she was a young woman that it takes away her breath. Ruth is also startled. It isn't just the fact that of all the women in the cove this should be the one at her father's door. It's more. Maud looks like an echo, so familiar that Ruth feels she must have had hundreds of long talks with Maud. She thinks that Maud is more of her mother than her own mother could ever be.

Neither one speaks until the pastor appears in the door. With a quick and stern hand he pushes Ruth away from the doorway and stares at Maud.

Not a word is spoken for a few moments. Maud is still dazed by seeing Ruth with the light of morning on her.

She sees the pastor is about to close the door so she reaches out and pushes her hand against the door. He tries to close it but Maud has more strength and he can't budge the door.

"Pastor, I can hold the door open all day, but I won't take long. 'Tis not for me I'm here."

He stops pushing the door, and Maud stands back.

"Sue is dead. I need you to give her a burying."

All the pastor does is shake his head.

"Because she was my friend?"

He nods and the door closes.

Maud is left alone.

Chapter Twenty-Two

Sue's body has been sewn into sail cloth. It lies in Maud's yard next to the painted beachrocks. The rain drifts across the yard. It clings to the stems of the flowers and drops from the petals. It beads in the grass and rolls down the beachrocks. Maud is in her oilskins and she is digging. The grave is almost finished. Rain sheens the shoulders and drips from the Cape Ann. The bottom of the grave hacked down past the shale is all mud and pools of sweet brown water. The spade crunches and splashes and as Maud heaves the mud past her shoulder the water sluices out of the mud and splashes down her back.

Now Maud climbs out of the grave up the small wooden ladder. She sticks the spade in the mound of earth and puts ropes under the small bundle of sailcloth that is Sue,

Maud stops to look at the cove in the rain. As she looks around she thinks of what Sue would never see again. She looks at the fog move in and start to hide the flakes and the store, the stage and the stage head and she listens to the fog horn as it wails and shakes the fog.

She thinks of Sue walking towards her house, she thinks of the way that Sue would smile when she came into the kitchen.

Now she just looks at the cove, and thinks as she looks at it that she's holding Sue's last memory.

She finishes with the ropes and wonders what she'll do to keep the body from splashing down into the grave, she wishes that she could clean the grave out and knows that all her strength was used up on what she'd done so far.

Maud does not want to cry today but she feels her eyes start to sting and for a moment she looks down at the earth and she leans on her spade.

When she looks up she sees Cavelle and Sarah. They look like part of a dream. Both float in the fog that has moved up to touch the house. Both carry yards of white cheesecloth in their arms.

Without saying anything Cavelle clambers down into the grave and Sarah passes down a bucket. They bail out the grave and all Maud can do is watch.

When the grave has been bailed out Cavelle climbs out and pulls up the small ladder. Sarah begins to unwrap a length of oilcloth and together she and Cavelle roll it down into the grave. It covers the ground. Then both throw in yards of cheesecloth. It billows like the top of combers, it folds like snow.

Cavelle and Sarah take two ropes and they look at Maud. Now she cries as she reaches out and takes the last rope.

They all place Sue into her new white bed. Then while Maud sobs they start to shovel the earth into the grave.

From the distance the fog horn blows. A passing steamer sounds its horn. The waves splash and the dirt splatters into the grave.

When they finish they smooth down the mound of earth like it was a comforter.

Cavelle and Sarah vanish into the fog.

Maud listens to the sound of rain on the earth.

Chapter Twenty-Three

I n the morning the sun hangs from a cloud. Vince and Pastor Roberts stand near the house of Maud. It holds in its trim the red of the sunlight and the small white picket fence holds the cloud.

Ruth sits on the green and yellow mixed grass at the edge of the fence and she chews on a long stem that strays near the gate. Her eyes are for the cloud as the sun slides behind it. The wind off the water picks up dark blue and black and rolls the cold of them towards Ruth. She pulls her sweater closer around her and folds up like a jack-knife. She looks at the ground and watches a bumble-bee nudge a flower.

Vince and the pastor make their way down to the stage head. There everything is still. All the boats are off to the fish and only the waves creak against the pilings. A scattered gull circles and mews when the two men arrive on the wharf but they pay no heed. The gull heads towards the sky and hooks a breeze that cups it towards the open sea. A few other gulls bob around in the swell that carries kelp in long brown streamers towards the shore. The tide is down and earlier kelp has been left to fade and crackle on the round beachrocks. Tin cans have washed up and an old engine rusts at the sky.

The skeleton of Uncle Mose Bugden's punt holds clusters of winkles on its ribs. The sun pokes through the clouds and wobbles shadows over the beach.

Vince and the pastor don't notice any of this. They look instead towards the house. As the sun comes out again the house catches the light and the windows do blink. Ruth leans back to feel the sun and her dress lies along her legs. The line of her body is lit as clearly as the house. Vince looks at her. The pastor looks at the house.

"'Tis perfect, Vince. The Lord himself has thrown the sunlight to show us the truth of the vision."

"If God wants us to build there, Pastor, then we will. The woman will soon leave and down comes the house, up goes the tabernacle."

"O praise the Lord. His bounty brings a harvest to the eyes."

Now the pastor takes paper and he sketches in the tabernacle as it will rise from the green earth. It is built in cubits and it will hold precious spices and cedar and trees from forests that hold the heat of midday and burn it into the hardest of woods. This house will go and the glory that is everlasting will be a rock for the shoreline.

"There will," he thinks, "be a series of mirrors and lights on the roof that will guide the boats." He will build a tunnel for the wind and it will howl a welcome to all sailors.

He looks at the pathway towards Maud's house and there next to the crushed cockleshells lies a conch shell. He goes to the gate, opens it, and picks up the conch. Vince watches the pastor lick his lips and raise the conch. The sun goes behind the cloud and a darkness comes upon the earth. Now there is fog and it is moving towards shore. As Vince and Ruth look towards the ocean a roll of fog tumbles faster and faster towards the shore.

The fog horn starts up and in counterpoint the pastor blows into the conch. His cheeks swell and his face goes red and a true and clear blast comes from the mouth of the shell. Again the fog horn. Again the conch.

The pastor knows he is calling the little boats to him. He blows again and again and walks towards the stage head. He takes a few steps and then he blows. He is always counterpoint to the fog horn, and it echoes around the cove. He blows long intense blasts and the sound butts its way through the fog bank. The wind shifts and blows on the back of the pastor. His long horn blasts are carried towards the fog.

With the wind turned around, the fog starts to blow away. The sun comes back and as fast as a running cat the fog scratches its way out to sea. The sun comes out and the beams fall on Ruth, she closes her eyes and lets the sun warm her body. Vince stares at the pastor.

The fog is gone, and he lowers the conch shell.

"The walls of Jericho, Vince. And the fog came tumbling down."

He walks back to the gate. Carefully he lays the conch to rest again.

"This be our cornerstone. A sign from the Lord."

The sun heats Ruth and she stretches like a cat in the sun.

Chapter Twenty-Four

It was a week later that Maud finished her work for Sue.

Sue had no relative who lived in the cove or near it so there was no question of what had to be done with her property. The whole cove knew there was a niece and the whole cove knew that everything should go to her. It didn't really make any difference that it was Maud who was settling everything. By now the whole cove also knew that the pastor had refused to bury Sue. Even the most ardent supporters of Pastor Roberts felt that there was something wrong. Not that a lot of people talked directly about it but some had started to nod a greeting towards Maud. Cavelle and Sarah were now talking to her and when it came time to cure the fish the scattered woman pitched in to help. Not when Maud was looking, but when she was out to sea. She'd come back and go to the flakes only to find out that her work was mostly done.

Now she was finishing looking after the last worldly goods of Sue. The house was dark. Maud had pulled down the blinds. So the house breathed in a deep cream colour and when the sun was bright the whole house was as light as a haystack.

It took Maud a while to find out the name and the address of the niece. No one had seen her for years. Sue had always talked a lot about the niece and told magic stories about what she was doing and about what she had said in her last letter. But when Maud went to look for the letters she couldn't find any.

That seemed strange because she found everything else. Whatever had been sent to Sue she'd kept. In drawer after drawer there were old Christmas cards, photos of people Maud didn't know, bills from the last decades and even pictures on faded scribbler paper. Maud looked at the pictures and found a name on them printed in childish handwriting. "Audrey" they said, and Maud knew that the niece's name was Audrey.

One of the pictures showed a small punt being rowed on what must have been a very blue sea. Now the crayon colour had faded and the blue sea lay under a powder white sky. An apple tree held small pink apples, and another boat sailed across the sky. Written in the sky as "To Ant Sue." Maud smiled and kept looking. Finally in the middle of the pile of bills she found one Christmas card from the niece. In the card she promised to write more often.

On that card there was an address so Maud knew where to send everything. She sent it collect because she wanted Audrey to think a little bit about her Aunt Sue.

Maud spent a long time building just the right crates out of pine and box-wood. She packed everything so it could never break even if the CN bunch did a dance on the crates or threw them all the way to Fort McMurray.

She spent a long time packing the crates because she stopped to look at everything. There was the tea set that held faded green flowers. The plates of lusterware. A huge blue willow pattern platter. Maud looked at it and thought as she always did of the lovers and their bridge. She packed crate after crate with dishes, lamps, pictures, lace doilies, and starched swans. Into the last crate she packed all the bills, letter, and cards. On top of everything she put the small picture to "Ant Sue." Then she shipped everything.

The strongest and best boards she saves till last. Maud has hammer and nails and she is boarding up the house of Sue. Inside, the empty house shakes and reverberates as the planks to the windows are bailed.

Finished, Maud stands back and looks at how clean and fresh the planks look.

She knows that the salt and the snow, the spring and the sun will turn the boards brown, then grey, and that in years to come the nail heads will rust and leave trails in jagged lines.

But for today the house looks crisp and packaged.

It looks like Sue has only gone away for a while.

The sun sets on the house as Maud stands in silhouette looking at her work. She turns and walks away and darkness moves to cover and hold the house of Sue.

Chapter Twenty-Five

Now Maud is in the early morning and she's drawn in deep black pencil against the grey sky.

Her shoulder heaves as she tries to start the one-lunger. Finally it catches and her boat begins to move away. It picks up speed and passes the sunkers.

Maud stands up and lets the wind blow round her face, it lifts the Cape Ann and only the chin strap keeps it from blowing away. The wind is up and the prow of the skiff lifts and splashes down into the waves. Gouts of water splash against the gunwales and a spray of salt water starts to cover Maud.

She looks at the teeth of the wind and feels her cheeks grow cold. Her lips start to split and she licks the salt into the cracks. She sniffs the wind and it's from the east and dirty. She keeps her course.

From the window of the pastor's house Vince is watching. The rain hits against the pane and runs down in tears. He hears the rain heavy and drumming on the roof. He watches Maud's boat until it's out of sight. Then he puts on a rain coat and without a word to anyone goes outside.

The rain hits his face and starts the cold moving and spreading as fast as he walks. The rain soaks his raglan and the damp moves on to his shoulders and his chest. He takes out a smoke and turning his back to the wind strikes a match. Four matches later he gets it going and drags in the taste of tobacco. As always in the damp it feels harsh. A raindrop lands on the cigarette and it sputters and the smoke tastes even more acrid. Vince flicks it into a puddle.

Now he is standing outside Maud's house. He looks around and sees that no one is near. He unlatches the gate and, leaving it open, moves towards the house.

It isn't locked. All that there is to do is pull on the string latch and feel the wood lever inside lift and the clunk of wood as the door swings open.

He stands in the outer porch. It is unpainted and shows some of the damp of the day. The linoleum is cracked and the floorboards have heaved so the floor itself is all a-tilt. There is an old washing machine stored there and a huge galvanized washtub against the wall.

Vince walks into the house and he feels the wash of memory. The kitchen tips him back and forth into and out of his childhood. At that moment he feels like walking away. All the blinds are still drawn, in memory of Sue, so he knows no one can see him. He raises the kitchen blind just a little and looks out. The wind blows rain at him and he moves back as it spatters the window.

Upstairs he stops in Maud's bedroom. He crosses the room and lies down on the bed. He feels it creak. He feels the feathers close around him. The ceiling holds painted boards and he looks at them.

He takes out his matches and he lights one. He holds it near the comforter and it is almost close enough to catch. He holds the match until it starts to burn his fingers. He flicks the flame out and gets up. He smoothes out the covers, and picks up a bit of ash.

Still cupping the burned-out match, he goes downstairs.

He lowers the blind again and walks towards the rain.

He closes the gate after him and only then does he throw down the burned out match.

The rain splashes on it.

All day and into the night the rain falls.

Chapter Twenty-Six

I t is night in the pastor's house and still the rain falls. Vince is smoking and pacing around his bedroom. The house is quiet. The pastor, his wife and sons had a prayer meeting around the arm and should have been back hours ago. Vince keeps listening for the sound of the motorboat that will bring back the family, and still he hears nothing.

The wind blows rain at the house and drips along the window sills. Under the door a damp patch creeps through the grain of the wood. Ruth has put a towel under the door and through the night it soaked up water. There is a leak in Vince's room and the double boiler is under it. At first the drips in the pan sounded like a dog's distant barking, now the sound is water on water and the plink of it is sharp on Vince's ears.

He moves towards his door and knows that the weather is too much. The pastor won't be home. He feels the blood beat against his ears and all he can hear is the rushing through his heart.

He walks along the hallway. The rushing joins a pounding like surf and it feels to Vince that he's being tumbled in a river as he nears the room of Ruth.

She is wide awake and all she can hear is the sound of creaking floorboards. The footsteps come slowly towards her door and then they stop outside. In the quiet of that moment she hears the rain against her window, she feels that rain cold against her heart. Then the door creaks open and a shaft of light lies upon the floor. Vince is carrying a lamp and all Ruth can see is the light from the lamp. Vince is nothing but a shadow. He stands in the doorway. Ruth is scared. She says nothing but lies there and pretends to be asleep even when Vince is saying her name. At first he says it softly then, as her eyes are shut as tight as tight can be, she hears the floorboards creak towards her and of a sudden his words are loud and hot in her ear.

She screams and smashes against his face and Vince reels back towards the door. The light trembles and goes out. There is one moment of terror and then, into the quiet, before Vince moves again there comes the sound of the motor boat, the propeller speeding and slowing as it leaves and plunges into the water. Closer. Closer.

The shadow shifts and Ruth is alone. She turns her face into the pillow and sobs deep so no one can hear her.

The wind starts to die down and the rain stops.

Chapter Twenty-Seven

On Monday the sun starts to suck water from all the puddles. Soon they dry and where there was wet mud now there is light yellow brown parched earth. As the day goes on the earth cracks more and more. The cod on the flakes smells like it's cooking and boys tear off small strips of the fish to chew like bubble gum.

The grass starts to dry and soon even the earth beneath and in between the grass is dry and hot to the touch. Out on the ocean the breeze has stopped and the sun bounces off the water. The forehead grows hot as the day goes on, necks turn red and faces flush. Old boats feel their boards creak and crack like ancient fingers towards the sun. Blinds are drawn and a heat that smells of wax spills through all the houses.

Horses look for trees and stand under them. Goats chew grass from the shady side of the hill. Some women go into their root cellars and just sit there. Milk spoils and in the houses blocks of ice melt steadily in the ice boxes. In the ice house the heat doesn't get past the sawdust on the blocks of ice. Old Roger Major has a lot of visitors in this heat and they all want to spend the day. He's kept busy loading blocks of ice into the cart and children try to chip off small knobs of ice to suck on. They grin and spit out the sawdust.

In the pastor's house the heat grows. It rolls over the big old stove in the kitchen and it rolls through the parlour. When the pastor plays "What a Friend We Have in Jesus" the organ sweats out the notes and his face is wet. Drops of sweat roll down his cheeks. But he blinks his eyes and keeps on playing. Ruth looks at her hymn book and the pages curl in the heat. Where she touches the page to follow the line with her finger wet licks the page.

Vince watches Ruth and knows she has said nothing about what happened. He expected to find her nervous. He was glad he did, and knew that it meant nothing. He knows that the next time she won't be scared.

He feels the heat creep under his shirt and he loosens his collar. The pastor's wife looks at Ruth and wonders what's wrong. She thinks that her daughter might be feeling the loosening of the grip of the Lord. That happens with time, she knows, and wants to find some way to let her daughter know that Jesus gets further away as the years go by. She doesn't know how to tell Ruth this and so she says nothing at all.

The heat shimmers in George's Cove and at night people lie on the tops of their beds. Windows are open but all that comes in is heat. People all pray for cool and ask their pillows for a breeze. They look at the moon and wonder why it gives off heat.

Wood dries. Along the beach the driftwood goes greyer and paler. Old trees turn blasty, the needles going from a faint green to a fiery orange red. The bark on the longers of the flakes turns light brown and curls and cracks.

Moss that's stuffed between boards to keep out rain and cold fades to a pale green and each fibre stands up like a hair does on cold hands.

The road through town leaves great still clouds of dust behind the pastor's truck. Because there is no wind the motes rise straight up and then are sucked along by the trail of the truck. Dust trembles and then settles in soft powder along the road and its banks.

The night shines moonlight through the dust motes and on the top of the moving truck. The white roof bounces back each moonbeam dusted pale.

In the pastor's house Vince is once more alone with Ruth. He walks to the door and pushes gently but the door will not yield. He pushes harder and hears a dresser scrape its legs and grip the floor and it throws the shadows upwards on his throat. The walls are swaying in yellow and orange and as Vince pushes harder at the door the light moon-tides it back and forth along the hall. Vince feels the sweat roll down his back and the door creaks open further and further and the lamplight glistens through the gap and lights up Ruth's face.

The shadows are catching in her eyes and her face is soft and lovely.

The door swings all the way open and the light is all upon Ruth. The heat and damp have pushed her nightgown against her breasts and her nipples stand out through the cloth. Vince smiles and moves when, in a grip of ice, a hand holds him by the neck and round he is turned to see the pastor.

The words that should have come to him don't and Pastor Roberts back-hands him across the face. Vince crashes to the wall and down and the lamp trembles light around the room. The hall shivers in the maze of shadows.

He grabs Vince and lifts him up and crashes him along the hall. Vince reaches for the outside door latch and is out into the night-time air. He is held by heat and moonlight. It shakes him loose against the house and he hears the door slam. Now he reaches in his pocket and tries to light a smoke. His hand shakes and the match won't stay lit. He turns away and walks from the pastor's house as it shimmers in the soft light.

Inside the pastor prays. He is on his knees in the study. On a table next to him are the plans and the model of the tabernacle. As if he's just hearing a whispered voice he gets to his feet and walks to the table of the model and the plans. With slow deliberate moves he crashes down his fist against the model of his tabernacle and it floats into pieces beneath his hand. The blue, the scarlet and the yellow all become splinters and grind to dust.

The pastor opens the small pot-bellied stove in his study. Despite the heat he strikes a match and lights the corners of the plans. He throws them into the stove and watches the corners curl to brown. Into the growing fire he throws the fragments of the tabernacle and it burns in a green flame. He closes the door of the stove and leans towards the heat.

His sweat hits the top of the stove and hisses, the fire comes through the grate in shadows that stripe the pastor's face.

Chapter Twenty-Eight

Vince is walking under the moon. His shoulders feel hot and his feet burn in the moon dust of the road. He stops to loosen his shoes and sits by the edge of the bank. The first hint of a wind blows along the road but it doesn't cool anything down. Instead it's as if someone opened a furnace.

He gets up and walks with the breeze. It takes him to the mouth of the cove. The heat pours off the shore and onto the water. The sea is still. The town is still and there is no sound except a distant dog howling towards the sky.

A cloud comes from nowhere and scuds across the face of the moon. For a moment there is a hint of cool and when the light comes out again it shines on Maud's stage. The shack holds moonlight which gathers on the roof and pours down the side and Vince is captured by the shine of it. He goes towards the old wooden door and opens it. The creak of the door crosses the cove, catches on a snag of rock and echoes back across the water. But Vince is now inside the shed.

The weighing scales are dusted by moonlight and shine like powdered apples. Nets are rolled into barrels and their weave is outlined by the light that shines through grimy windows. All is striped. The floor holds bold stripes crossed by obscure strips of moonlight.

In the corner there is a barrel used for tarring. It is crusted with old tar and it runs shiny around the rim. Vince goes close by and he lights his smoke. The tip of the cigarette glows and spins a circle of light into Vince's eyes. He holds the match and he looks at the tar barrel. As he looks the heat of the match reaches his fingers. He holds the match out and drops it. Flaring into the barrel it hisses and goes out.

He looks around until he sees a can of kerosene near the corner. Vince goes towards it and walks into the shadows.

Maud is only half asleep. She is dreaming of Ern falling from the scaffold. In her dream he falls and falls and (all-of-a-tumble) never reaches the ground. As he drops he catches fire and streaks soot and flame down the dark of the night. He calls out to her. He screams and Maud is flung from sleep.

She sits on the bed and puts her feet to the floor. She notices that it feels a little bit cooler and still scared and unable to get the thought of Ern from her mind she crosses to the window and looks out. The moon is full again but small clouds drift across it as Maud nods because the wind is coming up. The heat should soon be gone and she is about to turn back to bed when she glimpses something orange start to flicker in the window of the stage head. The clouds cross the moon again and as the moonlight dims the fire is clearer. Now it flutters at the window of her shed.

Vince is outside the stage head and he sits on the stage watching the fire start to lick at the window pane. Now it makes a low hiss as it moves into paint and then it makes a creak and a crackle as it licks off the paint and gets down to the wood. Vince smiles. His hand rests on the can of kerosene. He leans back and watches the fire start to grow. The distant dog has stopped howling and begins to bark. Some other dogs join in.

Suddenly, Maud rushes past him. She is running so fast that she doesn't look to one side or the other. She is wearing her nightgown and has it tucked haphazardly into her work pants. Vince is calm. It's like Maud is moving in slow motion.

In one hand she has a galvanized bucket on a rope. The rope is joined in a splice around the handle. In her other hand she grips a grey flannel blanket. She dips up bucket after bucket of sea water and dumps it into the cleaning tub. Then she drops the grey flannel blanket into the water and lets it start soaking. She dips up more water and begins to run towards the fire. On the wharf there is an old bell that's been there so long it's rusty, with the clapper glued to the side. She gives the bell a whack and then a few frantic clangs as she sets down the bucket. She picks it up again and splashes water on the fire and runs back and dips up more water. She throws it on the flames and the window blows outward.

Now Maud is ringing the bell again when she looks over and sees Vince sitting and watching the fire. She looks at him as the fire crackles and whistles.

"You son-of-a-bitch. You nothin'. You think this can touch me?"

She runs for more water. Vince stands up and throws kerosene on the flames. With a roar the fire leaps for the ceiling of the shed. Of a sudden, Maud grabs Vince and in a swirling sideways throw spins him off the wharf and through the burning door.

Now the heat is alive and it grabs Vince. It licks off sections of his jacket and smokes across his shoulders. It runs round his collar and singes the back of his hair. He cries and makes to run toward the door, toward Maud, but she splashes kerosene at the doorway and a sheet of flame flaps in the breeze.

Vince screams and cries. He's like a weasel darting towards the door and spinning back again.

He is weeping and Maud throws the kerosene at him again – but something is wrong, thinks Vince, 'cause it doesn't catch. She hits the flames with a blanket and Vince realizes that it's water and Maud is yelling at him to get out.

He leaps and of a sudden is outside and she whips the blanket over his shoulders and it burns with cold and he shivers at the edge of the wharf.

The water holds flame and licks orange at the moon that the new waves hold.

Maud looks at him as she stops trying to fight the fire.

"You wasn't worth killing, Vince."

Vince yells, "It would have been murder." And the hate of Maud fills him again and he seems to burn like the shed.

"Not killin' the likes of you. You can burn the whole place down and you can't touch me."

"I'll burn the house down."

"I'll build it again."

Vince looks toward the house and now he sees other faces. Faces lit by the fire. There's Amador and Obadiah, and people from the other side of the cove. He knows they heard everything. And Vince thinks he sees Ern at the edge of the crowd, but when he blinks Ern vanishes.

Amador looks at Vince, and Vince is about to explain when Amador turns from him. All the men and women join in and buckets are passed from hand to hand and even though the roof is falling in they keep passing the buckets along the line.

Vince has to go past them all. He walks with the blanket steaming on his shoulders and no one looks at him. All the children, all the mothers and fathers help Maud put out the fire.

Vince walks away and only once does he look back. He sees the fire and he sees the line of people and he knows that he has lost.

He finds a root cellar door open and he goes inside to the cool where he sleeps.

Chapter Twenty-Nine

It is morning. The day is cool and grey.

Because it doesn't look like rain some of the women are hanging out clothes to dry. The clothes-pins hold garments to dangling wires and the wind blows sheet shapes into the line.

Children walk on stilts. They weave back and forth across the road. The stilts make small dents in the ground. Some boys drag their stilts. They make thin lines of dust which the wind blows away.

From houses near the shoreline comes the smell of fresh baked bread. Small children lean in doorways waiting for a taste.

Near the cove the smell is of smoke and water.

Most of the boats have gone out for the morning but the *Maud & Me* is still tied up to the wharf.

Maud and Cavelle and Sarah are all at the stagehead. They are dragging away the debris and heaving it over the wharf. They work together and they say no words.

Vince is at the government wharf. He waits for the steamer and his hands are covered with bandages. His hair sticks out and looks singed. He looks at his feet and the wind blows around him.

The steamer's whistle blows and a small boat comes in from it to pick up Vince.

As Maud throws a burned piece of timber into the water she looks and sees Vince board the boat.

He doesn't look back. Not when he gets on the little boat, not when he boards the steamer and not when it steams down the arm.

Maud walks towards Cavelle and Sarah.

She thinks that's enough work for the day.
She decides to ask them to tea in her house.
Maud's House.

Epilogue

In her dream Ern was young.
He was naked and splashed in the river.
In the sand lay his saw and he stretched his hand toward it. Like a snapped painter it flew towards him and was in his hand.
He swam beneath the water and Maud, watching, took off all her clothes.
She found Ern sitting cross-legged near some waving reeds. He buckled the saw till the light from the water started to play it.
It played her song and Maud started singing. Her voice and the sound of the saw under water spun the light in crazy colours like her great grandmother's windows.
Everything was a rainbow.
Everything was music.
Everything was a song that they sang together.
The water rang and the sun chimed as Ern and Maud floated out to sea.